Mel Foster
and the
TIME MACHINE

JULIA GOLDING

Mel Foster and the TIME MACHINE

EGMONT

EGMONT

We bring stories to life

First published in paperback in Great Britain 2016
by Egmont UK Limited
The Yellow Building, 1 Nicholas Road, London W11 4AN

Text copyright © 2016 Julia Golding
Illustrations copyright © 2016 Pete Williamson

The moral rights of the author and illustrator have been asserted

ISBN 978 1 4052 7971 0

www.egmont.co.uk

62457/1

A CIP catalogue record for this title is available from the British Library

Typeset by Avon DataSet Ltd, Bidford on Avon, Warwickshire
Printed and bound in Great Britain by the CPI Group

For Toby

Contents

Chapter One
Stop, Thief!

Buckingham Palace, London, 1895

Mel Foster did not consider himself an expert on royalty, but even he knew there was something horribly wrong with the queen. Victoria had just walked past where he stood among the guests at this special reception and stepped out on to the balcony of Buckingham Palace to wave to the crowds. As Mel took his seat with the rest of the audience, he watched her through the glass doors. At first she had appeared very much as her subjects expected: a stout little figure with a pale oval face, dressed in black, and bedecked in jewels. But when Mel blinked and looked again, he saw that there was now something seriously amiss with her crown and Mel really, *really* did not want to be the one to tell her.

1

Meanwhile in another palace, St Petersburg, Russia . . .

The new Tsar of Russia breezed into the imperial family's breakfast room, a footman two paces behind carrying a casket bound with an emerald ribbon. Outside the first autumn frost had laced all the leaves in the court garden. The blue sky gave the pale walls of the palace a fairytale glow. Inside, the splendour continued with the gilt and cream ornamentation, floor-to-ceiling mirrors and crystal chandeliers. At the heart of this setting was the Tsar's most precious gem: his young wife, Alexandra, sipping on a cup of chocolate, golden hair gleaming in a shaft of sunlight. He was delighted to see that her expression brightened on his entrance.

'I have just heard from my ambassador in London,' Nicholas announced, putting aside her cup and kissing her fingertips, 'and it's good news, my sweet. Your royal grandmother Queen Victoria has recovered from her dangerous infatuation with that butler fellow and he has been sent on his way. England is returning to normal, except, that is, for the presence of those monsters.'

Alexandra shuddered, her big blue eyes round with alarm. 'Oh, Nicholas, I don't think I could bear to live surrounded by those creatures. There aren't any in Russia, are there?'

He patted her hand. 'Let's hope we never find out. And learn the lesson not to let some dangerous fellow get too much influence over us.' Nicholas believed he might be surrounded by quite a few monsters but thought it safest not to tell his wife in her delicate condition. Their first child was due any day. 'Now, to celebrate, I've had Fabergé make you a special egg for this morning's breakfast.'

The footman held out the casket.

'Is that for me?'

'Oh yes, my love. They tell me it is the most expensive one Fabergé has ever made – a little mechanical toy with golden parts and diamond inlay, celebrating the downfall of that evil butler.' Taking the box from the footman, the Tsar placed the gift in her lap. 'Go on: open it, little mouse.'

As Alexandra paused for a second to enjoy her anticipation, there was a sudden blur of movement in the room – the flap of a muslin curtain by an open window. The silk fringe on the empress's dress fluttered. 'Oh, what was that? Has a pigeon got in?' she asked.

'I don't know.' The Tsar scanned the painted ceiling but cherubs continued their cheerful riot undisturbed. 'Guards: check the windows.'

While his bodyguard carried out his order, Nicholas turned back to his gift. 'Where were we? Your Fabergé egg.'

His wife smiled up at him. 'Ah yes.' She plucked the emerald ribbon but it had become knotted. 'Oh you silly: you left it in a tangle!'

The Tsar looked affronted. 'I certainly did not.'

Laughing softly, she lifted the lid. Her expression hovered between dismay and curiosity, unsure which she should feel. 'Oh.'

'What!' The Tsar couldn't believe the evidence of his own eyes. Instead of a gem-encrusted egg, a pineapple lay on the red silk lining.

'Is this it?' asked Alexandra, reaching out a slim fingertip to feel the rough skin. 'It's certainly the most realistic Fabergé has made yet.'

'Stop!' cried the Tsar, pulling the box away from her. 'Don't touch it, heart-of-mine! Guards, get the empress to safety.'

Alexandra rose unwillingly as the bodyguards hastened to help her from her seat. An elbow made contact with her cup and chocolate spilled over the pristine tablecloth, forming a stain oddly like the shape of Russia. 'But whatever is wrong, my love?'

'There's a thief in the palace.' The Tsar whirled through the room, overturning chairs and side tables. He yanked down the curtains to reveal an empty balcony outside the room. 'Search everywhere, men! Find the egg and punish the wrongdoer! I will not have my palace invaded like this!'

But even the most thorough search ever undertaken in a thousand years of Russian history could not turn up the missing Fabergé egg. The jewel thief had escaped, leaving no clue as to his identity behind.

Meanwhile back in London . . .

The two soldiers either side of the open balcony door had their backs to the monarch, eyes on the extraordinary gathering of monsters and other guests in the chamber. The queen was for the moment alone with her people before she invited her family to join her. Mel held his breath to head off the giggle bubbling up in his chest, thinking that if it worked for hiccups it should work for laughter. He and the others from the Monster Resistance had been invited to this ceremony at the palace to receive awards for saving the Empire from the Demon Butler. He had to behave.

Misjudging her strength, Eve Frankenstein nudged Mel, causing him to tumble off his chair. She plucked him effortlessly from the floor and brushed off his smart black uniform before reseating him. Mel and Eve were placed closest to the balcony doors and could clearly see the masses gathered on the Mall in front of the palace, a pebble beach of upturned faces.

'*Excusez-moi*, Mel Foster, but is Her Majesty really wearing what I think she is wearing?' asked Eve in a low voice.

'Yes, Eve. The queen appears to be wearing a crown topped by an orange.'

'Shall we alert the others?' Eve asked.

The Jekyll twins, Cain and Abel, sat two rows in front, heads close together – one set of neatly combed locks touching the other's bristly tufts. Next to them, sharing a single seat, perched the little monster fairies Nightie and Inky, both absorbed in admiration of their new dresses cut from purple satin and edged with ermine. Nightie was spitting on his boots to bring them to a high gloss; Inky was comparing the bangles on his knobbly wrists. Lady Viorica Dracula was seated demurely beside them like a girl at her first tea party, her blood-red gown settled elegantly around her ankles, gaze fixed on the neck of a bewigged footman standing by the wall. The vampire was hungry.

'Or maybe should we tell the queen first?' asked Eve.

'Probably.' So far out of everyone gathered for the ceremony, it appeared only Mel and Eve had seen that instead of the Second Star of Africa, the diamond that normally sat at the peak of the Imperial Crown, Her Majesty now sported a fruit. It was doing an admirable job of filling the gap, Mel admitted, but wasn't quite up to the standard of the priceless gem it had replaced.

Meanwhile in the Louvre, Paris, France . . .

'*Non, non,* Monsieur Monet, I do not think the Mona Lisa so very intriguing,' said Auguste Renoir, renowned portrait artist. 'I agree that her eyes follow you around the room, but she has no vitality. I prefer my models to be more,' he searched for a word, caressing his beard, 'unexpected.'

Revolving the brim of his battered felt hat in his fingers, Claude Monet, leading light of the impressionist painters, contemplated the most famous picture in the world. 'I rarely attempt a portrait myself. The impossibility of exceeding this one always haunts me. Ah, what the great Leonardo knew about painting! We stand in the long shadow of his reputation.'

Renoir frowned. He privately rather thought he had made great strides out of da Vinci's shade with his latest exhibition. 'But still we must attempt it, I hope you agree?' He massaged his hands, feeling a twinge of arthritis set off by a cold draught. There must be an open window somewhere, he decided.

'Indeed, we must. Yet how you can claim she has no vitality, I do not know.' Monet gestured to the famous smile. 'She always looks to me as if she could jump off the wall and run away with the kitchen boy – she has that mischievous twinkle in her eye.'

A breeze ruffled the long wisps of Monet's white beard. A shape flitted across the painters' vision, like the uncertain light trembling on the surface of a lily pool.

Renoir blinked. '*Sacré bleu!* What was that?'

'*Non!* I don't believe it! She has gone!' cried Monet.

Both painters stared aghast at the spot where until a second ago had hung the Mona Lisa. In its place dangled a picture made up of fruit – not painted fruit, but *real* fruit, nailed haphazardly to a plank. In the place of the

Mona Lisa's smile there now grinned a banana.

'This is sacrilege! Someone is thumbing their nose at us!' exclaimed Monet.

'Guards!' bellowed Renoir. 'Hurry!'

'Stop thief! Lock the doors – stop them getting away!'

Yet though every visitor to the Louvre was thoroughly searched, and the gendarmes deployed in force around all ports and railway stations to check baggage, the Mona Lisa was not found. She did indeed appear to have jumped off the wall and run away of her own accord.

And in London . . .

Eve swivelled her brown eye, then her blue to study Queen Victoria. Made from patched together bodies of deceased orphan girls, Eve's features occasionally worked independently from each other as if they recalled their previous separate existence.

'Before Her Majesty left the room, I seem to remember there was a gemstone there, no?' She tapped her head. At over seven feet tall, Eve made an impression on anyone who met her. It was tempting to be scared of the rather alarming way she was sewn together, that was until you realized her heart was pure kindness.

Mel nodded, his urge to laugh thankfully fading as the seriousness of the situation sank in.

'But I also think I remember there being a blur in the corner – something dashing towards the queen – then it disappeared. Poof! Like that.' Her handclap reverberated like thunder, briefly drawing all eyes, before the courtiers glanced away, not yet over their fear of the giantess.

'Yes, Eve, we have a citrus emergency,' agreed Mel. 'We can't let the queen stand out there like that; she'll be so embarrassed later.' Mel got up, rubbing his temples. His memory, like Eve's, was struggling with two versions of what had happened. In one the queen had progressed out to the balcony quite undisturbed; in the second he had seen the blurred shape Eve described. The images moved in his brain like two trains on parallel tracks running at the same speed until they reached a junction where the two trains miraculously became one. And that one had a fruit, not a diamond, on board.

'Go on then.' Eve lifted Mel over her legs like he was a parcel for delivery and stood him in the aisle. 'She likes you.'

'She might not feel that way much longer.' Bracing himself, Mel walked to the door and coughed discretely.

Out in the fresh air, the queen carried on waving, enjoying the applause of her subjects, all so pleased to see her restored to health now the wicked butler was gone.

Mel coughed louder. Mr Copperfield, the queen's

private secretary, tottered over, his bushy white hair sprouting in exuberant fashion over his friendly old face. 'Master Foster, is there a problem?'

'Look at the queen, sir,' whispered Mel. '*Really* look, I mean.'

The old man's jaw dropped. 'Your Majesty!' he squawked.

This the queen did hear. She turned towards them. 'Yes, Copperfield? What is it? Is it time to start the ceremony?'

'No, Your Majesty – I mean, yes, Your Majesty. Oh, Your Majesty!' Mr Copperfield fell to wringing his hands.

Mel decided to put his friend out of his misery. 'Ma'am, there's been a wardrobe . . . um . . . muddle.'

'Whose?' she asked.

'Yours?' suggested Mel carefully.

'What do you mean, young man?' Queen Victoria's little eyes narrowed in disapproval of his boldness.

There really was no way to say this without being blunt. Best get it over with. 'You are wearing an orange rather than a diamond on the top of your crown.'

'What!' Her hand flew up to check. Touching the fruit, she whipped back inside, snapping her fingers at her ladies-in-waiting. 'Lady Louise, Lady Anne – remove this abomination at once!'

Startled, the ladies flocked to her side and lifted the heavy crown from her head, giving crows of distress.

They placed it on a blue cushion, where it had nested before the event began. A cuckoo had got into the rookery.

'Why is there an orange on one's crown!' demanded the queen.

'Stop thief!' shouted Mr Copperfield, coming to his senses. 'Lock the doors! Search everyone!'

Two spots of red appeared high on Her Majesty's cheeks. 'You let one appear on the balcony with that on one's head! How dare you!'

'Your Majesty – I didn't – we didn't . . .' spluttered Mr Copperfield. 'It wasn't there before!'

'We most certainly are not amused.' With a stamp of a royal foot, the queen stalked out of the throne room.

There was an embarrassed silence.

Mel poked the orange. 'Looks like we won't be getting any awards today after all.'

Mr Copperfield nodded glumly. 'Turn out your pockets, everyone. No one leaves until that diamond is found.'

But it wasn't to be found in anyone's possession, or hidden in the room, despite a thorough search.

One of the most important gems in the Crown Jewels was missing.

Chapter Two

The Hunchback of Regent's Park

The night of the thefts, the Monster Resistance held an emergency meeting at their base in the Jekyll twins' home. Theirs was a house of two parts. At the front, facing the elegant Bloomsbury square, it was everything you would expect of a London gentleman's residence: tall windows, black railings and immaculate paintwork. The mews at the rear told a different story, as there the Jekylls had their stables and workroom – low brick buildings suited to messy experiments and oily machinery. The Resistance members had been summoned to the hush of the dining room on the first floor, with its heavy red velvet drapes blocking out the sounds of the square beyond. Mel felt a shiver of anticipation as he entered the candlelit chamber and took his place in the middle of the long mahogany table. The candelabra reflected in the polished surface, each taper a little lighthouse in the darkness. The room was full of mysteries and it was as well the curtains were closed so no one could look in on the incredible inhabitants of the house, all of whom were peculiar in their own unique ways.

Cain and Abel's secret was that they were able to exchange bodies at will, a fluke of nature inherited from their unfortunate father, the original Dr Jekyll. They often squabbled as to who was going to enjoy the freedom and brute strength of the larger body, as opposed to the elegance of the other. Cain had won the argument that evening so was sitting with his feet up on the table, scratching his belly through a gap in his shirt, slouched in the carver chair at the far end near the fireplace. His jug ears sprouted dark hair and his jaw looked quite capable of taking a punch or two – the appearance of a thorough thug and playground bully, as he'd once admitted cheerfully to Mel. His brother, Abel, sat with a student prince's poise at the opposite end, his lush light-brown locks flowing in artistic waves to his collar, his clothes immaculate, his features the kind young ladies swooned over.

A bat fluttered in at a high window and circled the room.

'Ah, excellent, our last member has arrived. Shall we get started?' said Abel, opening the ledger in front of him.

Viorica materialized from bat form to girl behind one of the curtains. She emerged wearing the black satin dressing gown left there for her convenience. Her hair was a little windswept from her recent flight, still turning from bat grey to blonde. By the time she was seated, all was sleek. 'Good evening, fellow monsters. I have most curious news about the thefts.'

Abel took up his gold-nibbed fountain pen. 'Excellent, Lady Viorica. But first let us take our roll call.' A boy of methodical scientific habits, Abel had insisted they start keeping proper records now they were a legitimate organization and had been acknowledged by the queen herself as the last line of defence against threats to her Empire. 'Cain Jekyll?'

'Here, *obviously*,' said his brother. 'You can see me, can't you?' Cain had more slapdash habits compared to Abel and wasn't a fan of the register. He said it felt too much like school – a place both Jekylls had studiously avoided attending.

Ignoring the jeer, Abel made a note. 'Lady Viorica Dracula?'

'Present.' Viorica had taken her place at Abel's right hand and now accepted the cup of ox blood that he poured for her from a teapot.

Abel smiled at her, keeping his frowns for the others. 'I kept it warm for you.'

Ugh. Mel had noticed that Viorica and Abel were a little sweet on each other. Still they had a lot in common with the whole transformation thing and ruthless nature. Must be odd for Cain though. Mel glanced at his friend at the far end. Cain was cracking nuts between thumb and forefinger then flicking the shells at the family portraits that hung on the walls, paying no attention to his brother.

'Mademoiselle Eve Frankenstein,' continued Abel.

'*Oui.*' Eve was sitting quietly in her chair at Mel's side. She had broken quite a few items of furniture in the Jekyll household before they made her own suitably reinforced set. This chair was carved with scenes of the Polar north, bears and igloos. Her father had raised Eve there until she had become lost in the ice and revived sixty years later by Mel.

'Raven?'

'*Nevermore*!' squawked the bird from the top of the bust of Plato. It was his only word and served to express everything from 'I want a beetle' to 'Run for your lives'. Cain flipped him a nut, which the bird caught with a click of his beak.

'Incubus Fairy?'

Inky scrambled out from under Mel's chair, hauled himself up Eve's skirt and sat on the table cross-legged. 'All shipshape and Bristol fashion, sir.'

Abel sighed. 'A simple "yes" would do. Nightmare Fairy?'

Nightie climbed up Mel's trouser leg and joined his brother. From the icing sugar dusting and trail of string from his mouth, Mel deduced that the fairies had been snacking under the table on sugar mice. 'Huh-umm.' Nightie swallowed. 'Sir.'

'Mummy?'

The lid to a splendid golden sarcophagus standing upright by the door creaked open. The Egyptian mummy stepped out and bowed. He had been accidentally reanimated by an archaeologist and now served as cook and driver to the household. His mummified cat followed, leaping up on to Eve's lap for a stroke, her stiff tail pointing up like a fire poker.

'Jacob Marley?' No response. Abel looked up.

'It's nighttime, sir,' Mel reminded him. 'He's out with the other ghosts "bewailing his manifold sins" and carrying his chains and cashboxes.'

'Oh yes.' Abel put the household butler's name under Absences. 'I've also received apologies from our two honorary human members, Dr Foster and Mr Copperfield. Dr Foster was worried it might rain so stayed home. Mr Copperfield is dealing with the emergency at the palace. So that leaves . . . Melchizedek Foster.'

'Present.' Mel winked at Cain, who rolled his eyes at his brother's love of process.

'Good. Now we can hear the report.' Abel closed the register.

Mel put up a hand.

'Yes, Master Foster?' asked Abel.

'What about you, sir? Aren't you going to call your own name?'

Cain chuckled at Mel's cheek.

'I've already marked myself present,' said Abel. 'Now, if we may proceed without further interruptions. My lady?'

Viorica sipped from her cup. 'I have come directly from Scotland Yard. The police have no leads on the thief beyond the statements already given by Mademoiselle Frankenstein and Mel Foster. They were the only ones to see anything.'

'But we didn't see much,' admitted Mel.

'And that is the strangest part of the whole affair,' said Abel, jotting on a piece of paper a few thoughts.

'Ah, but it isn't, Abel my sweet. As I hung from the ceiling – they have a very useful rafter over the post room – I heard telegraph reports arriving from other countries. The Tsar's finest Fabergé egg was stolen this morning – as was the Louvre's Mona Lisa. There is a reward offered for the return of both items.'

'*C'est incroyable!*' exclaimed Eve.

'An incredible day indeed, but what do they have to do with the Second Star of Africa?' asked Abel.

Viorica delicately patted her mouth with a linen napkin.

'In each case the thief entered and left with no trace.'

'Thieves, surely? How can you be in three places at once?' asked Eve.

'Exactly: it's impossible. Go on, my lady,' said Abel.

'But the most telling common factor of the robberies is that, in each case, fruit was left behind.' The vampire's eyes sparkled with amusement.

'Oranges?' asked Mel.

'No, a pineapple in Russia, and a fruit picture with a banana mouth in Paris, each suiting the nature of the object stolen.' Viorica gave her own enigmatic smile, looking for a second like the Mona Lisa's younger sister. 'You have to admit that this gang of thieves has style.'

'Can't be coincidence,' said Cain, voicing everyone's thoughts. 'This has to be a coordinated attack – three thieves set to steal Europe's most precious objects, leaving the gang signature behind: a piece of fruit.'

'That appears to be a message – but of what kind?' mused Abel.

'I think it says that we – the people guarding the goods – are bananas,' said Mel.

'And we certainly are left looking foolish. We were all there – the royal family, government, soldiers, the Monster Resistance – and still the queen was left with an orange on her head,' agreed Abel.

'Do you think it was him – the Inventor?' asked Mel, rubbing the key-shaped scorch mark on his chest, relic of his father's experiments. He would never forget the moment they discovered that his father, a shadowy figure who styled himself 'the Inventor', had been the mastermind behind the plot to put a butler in charge of the British Empire. Mel had not met him and hoped their paths would never cross.

'It certainly bears his hallmark of fiendish cleverness and desire to overturn those in power,' said Abel.

'But the comic element seems off, don't it?' threw in Cain. 'He's never shown anything but deadly seriousness before.'

'True. But we should put him on our list of suspects.' Abel made a note. 'He could still be behind it.'

'Have we been asked to investigate?' Mel had noticed an official looking letter on the table next to the ledger.

Abel nodded, tapping the envelope. 'Most insistently, by the queen herself. But we won't be the only ones. Every policeman, military officer and private detective has been asked to turn their mind to the problem. She is calling in her best trackers from all corners of the Empire. Sherlock Holmes has already examined the scene of the crime and said that he has eliminated the impossible, and what remains is so improbable even he cannot believe it is true.'

'Which is?'

'A jest by Her Majesty. She was the only one close enough to make the switch, he claims.'

Cain guffawed. 'He's lost his marbles if he thinks that.'

'As I said, he didn't believe his own deduction so went home to Baker Street defeated.'

Cain cracked his knuckles. 'So we have a mystery that has stumped the great Sherlock himself. Let's have a go then.'

'Ideas, anyone?' Abel looked round the table.

Mel searched his brain but found only a grey blur. 'Someone very, very fast?'

His idea wasn't booted out of play as he expected. 'Possible.' Abel wrote it down. 'We'll have to ask if any of our monster friends have such a power. Viorica, you are the swiftest of us: could you have done it?'

The vampire tapped a fingernail against a fang in thought. 'Even for me that is too fast. I could reach the crown quickly but to replace the diamond without anyone noticing? I think not.'

The mummy waved his hand, brown bandage trailing.

'Yes, Mummy?'

The mummy began a little pantomime, sticking his arms out in front of him and striding across the room.

'Mesmerism?' guessed Eve as the cat butted her hand for more strokes.

The ancient Egyptian nodded vigorously.

'All of us at once? I don't recall losing consciousness

at all. My recollection is exact and in one piece,' said Abel. 'What do you all remember?'

'Same,' grunted Cain. 'But we weren't looking directly at her.'

'Eve and I were,' said Mel. 'We remember . . . well, confusion. Two competing memories with and without fruit.'

'That must be significant – but not a sign that you were hypnotized, I think.' Abel noted this down in the Dubious Theory column.

'It's obvious what that leaves,' said Cain.

'It is?' asked Mel.

'Yes, magic.' Cain's green eyes twinkled.

Abel wrote it down then struck it out. 'No, magic is just natural processes not yet given a scientific explanation.'

'Go on then, brother: explain.' Cain crushed another nut.

Abel gave a humph.

'Got you there.' Cain swept the shell into the palm of his hand and gulped that down too. 'Let's see if we can come up tomorrow with anything better than a very fast thief or a wizard at loose in London.'

'And we have the other thefts to consider. I think a quick visit to the scenes of the crime are in order,' added Abel. 'Best pack a bag, Cain.'

A few days later, Mel's slumbers were interrupted at three in the morning by an insistent knocking on the door.

The ghost butler, Jacob Marley, was present to answer the summons. Mel lay in the darkness listening to the muffled sounds below, wondering what was going on.

'Oh, sir, we have an emergency!' Marley wailed as he drifted up through the floor of Mel's bedroom and continued to the ceiling and on up to the top floor.

Mel hopped out of his warm sheets and quickly located his clothes in a heap on the floor. 'What's happened, Mr Marley?'

But the ghost had already floated on to the other chambers.

'You won't find the twins,' Mel called after him. 'They're in Paris, remember! And Viorica's doing whatever a vampire does at night.'

Inky and Nightie stuck their heads out from under Mel's bed. 'Are we needed too, Mel?' asked Nightie, his pink striped nightcap drooping over one eye, black beard in curlers.

'Probably not. I'll give you a shout if you are.'

'Righto,' said Inky with a yawn, snuggling back under the doll's quilt they used for bedding.

As a last thought, Mel fixed his M entwined with an R diamond badge in his lapel, official sign of a member of the Monster Resistance, and took a shortcut down the polished banister to the entrance hall, landing with a little thump of boot soles on chequered tiles. Marley returned with Eve.

'Mr Marley, please stop fussing about doom and

danger and tell us why you've dragged us out of bed?' asked Mel.

'There are policemen, sir. On the doorstep.' The butler's ghostly chain wrapped round him like a boa constrictor, a sign of his distress. 'Two of them.'

Mel cast a quick look at Eve. 'Have you done anything worthy of arrest recently?' Since becoming part of the Monster Resistance, they'd both become more used to doing things that weren't strictly within the law – all in the interests of the Empire of course. Eve shook her head. Mel remembered the housebreaking lessons Cain had given him last week but no one had caught them at it – at least not yet. 'Then let's hear what they have to say.' He threw open the door. 'Morning, all. What's this all about then?'

The police sergeant jumped at Mel's sudden appearance on the doorstep. His eyes further widened when he spotted Eve and the ghost bobbing behind her. Mel noticed that the man's handlebar moustache looked a little ragged, indicating he had passed the time waiting chewing worriedly on the ends. 'Apologies for disturbing you, sir and . . . er . . . madam, but we have a little problem at the zoo.'

'Quite a big problem really, lady and gents,' chipped in an alert young constable at the sergeant's shoulder who by contrast was enjoying the sight of the unusual inhabitants of the house. Society was divided into those few who enjoyed the coming out of monsters into the public eye and the majority who feared them. The two policemen evidently represented both schools of thought. 'Cor, are you a real ghost?' the constable asked Mr Marley. 'I'm tickled pink to meet you.'

'Quiet, Wilkins,' warned his superior officer.

'Can you be a little more specific about the nature of your problem?' asked Mel.

'It might be best if you see for yourselves.' The sergeant gestured to the waiting police van.

Mel laughed. 'Oh no. I'm not getting in a van without knowing who sent you and why. Our address is supposed to be secret.'

'It is, sir – only given out in an emergency to trusted officers at Scotland Yard,' said the sergeant, adopting an air of great self-importance.

'So why now?'

'You were recommended by Mr Copperfield,' blurted out the irrepressible Wilkins, 'because you're monsters and speak French.'

'Wilkins!' growled the sergeant.

'But it's true, sir.'

'Yes, but we were also instructed to be tactful.'

Catching Eve's eye, Mel checked she was in agreement. 'All right, officer,' said Mel, 'we'll come with you to the zoo, but in our own vehicle. We'll meet you there.'

Eve went off to the dining room to knock on the sarcophagus.

The sergeant rocked on his heels pompously. 'Right you are, sir. I'll make sure there's someone to show you the way when you get to the zoo.'

Regent's Park zoo was a short drive away at that time of night on empty roads. The mummy pulled up the horseless carriage, or motorcar as the twins called it, outside the main entrance. Leaves rattled in the light breeze. The occasional exotic hoot or howl marked out that these railings surrounded more than just an ordinary park. Creatures from all over the world were packed into the zoo, living uneasily side by side, predator and prey.

The police van was already waiting by the ticket kiosk, the horses feeding peacefully from a nosebag under the care of Wilkins, who stood scratching their ears, whistling tunelessly.

'So, Constable, where's the problem?' asked Mel.

'In the bear enclosure, sir,' said Wilkins.

'Will you show us the way?'

'I'm afraid I've been ordered to attend the horses, sir.'

'Why?' asked Mel, sensing a story.

'Apparently I'm to stop them running away as I can't stop my tongue. Sergeant Bolter has left a zookeeper to greet you.'

'Bad luck.'

Wilkins gave him a quick grimace. 'It ain't fair. It's a prime monster in that cage and I'm missing all the fun.'

At those intriguing words, the zookeeper stepped out of the nearest building. 'Follow me, sir, madam.'

They passed under the wrought iron archway and into the labyrinth of enclosures and cages beyond. Trees rustled, a sleepy undertone to the squawks and groans that emerged from the boxlike pavilions. The air smelt of elephant dung.

Eve shivered. 'I don't like this place, Mel Foster. Why do they put bars around the creatures?' She had narrowly escaped being put on display herself when she had first been discovered in the ice.

'The animals are too dangerous to let loose,' explained Mel.

'Then why not leave them in their homes where they can run free?'

That was a good question and Mel was sure there was a complicated answer about study and education but all replies flew from his brain when they stopped by the bear enclosure at the spot where the policemen had gathered. Sergeant Bolter had brought a party of six with him, clearly expecting trouble. Softly lit by moonlight, a family of brown bears was huddled at one end, the mother growling and swiping the air, protesting at the invasion of their space. At the other end was a large misshapen bundle of clothes bent over a crate of fruit. From time to time, a hand would emerge from the cloak to take out a banana, apple or pear and chuck it towards the bears. The creature muttered something gruffly in a language that might be French.

Mel tugged Eve's sleeve. 'What's he saying?'

'I think he's asking why they won't be friends,' Eve whispered, 'but he speaks oddly.'

A pear hit the mother bear on the nose. 'Perhaps they won't because he's got terrible aim?' Mel moved closer to the bars. 'What is he?'

The sergeant folded his arms. 'That, young sir, was rather what we were hoping you could tell us.'

'Eve, why don't you speak to him?' prompted Mel.

But the suggestion came too late. The creature threw another pear at the mother bear and she decided she had had enough. From sitting, she suddenly upped and charged towards him, growling deep in her barrel chest.

'Oh no!' gasped Mel.

It looked like the creature was going to be mauled before their very eyes but he surprised them all by evading the bear with a leap to grasp the top of the enclosure bars. Swinging from hand to hand, nimble as a chimpanzee, he made his way to the far end, chattering a stream of French insults at the angry bear.

'Quick, it's getting away!' shouted Sergeant Bolter. 'Riflemen, stand ready!' Two of his men shouldered their guns, setting their sights on the fleeing figure.

'*Non*, no shooting!' said Eve, dumping her coat. 'I fetch him!'

The creature had now made a huge leap from the

27

bear enclosure into the elephants' next door. He was very agitated, running with a strange lopsided gait, bent almost all the way over to use his hands as well as his feet. The elephants, which had been sleeping in a huddle, began to trumpet and shift with alarm.

'Stop! *Arrête!*' called Eve.

That only spurred the creature on to greater efforts to escape. He climbed up the leg of the nearest elephant and ran along the backs of the little herd. Trunks flew up, trying to swipe him off, but he dodged each one. Taking a rolling jump, he went up and over the wall to the path beyond.

'Where's he going now?' wondered Mel as he chased after Eve.

'I think he go for the gate. *Excusez-moi!*' Eve put on a burst of speed and leapt on to the nearest elephant, taking it to its knees. She didn't even dodge the trunks, ignoring the slaps as if they were no more than gentle taps.

The creature, meanwhile, jumped over the fence into the giraffe pen, sprang up and spun around the neck of the tallest one, then sling-shotted himself into the monkey house. Arms and legs spread mid-flight, he landed safely on a tree stump in the centre of the enclosure. Howler monkeys responded to his arrival with ear-splitting cries. They rushed towards the intruder, but he dived away, swinging from rope to rope as the troop gave chase. The boy – for Mel could see now the creature's cloak had flapped open that it was a boy – was amazingly agile, out-twisting, out-jumping the zoo's most nimble inhabitants.

Eve leapfrogged the giraffes and landed in the centre of the monkey enclosure. Outraged, the howlers dropped on her, screaming in her ears, pulling her hair, but she just brushed them off.

'*Taisez-vous, petits singes,*' she said, barely paying them any attention. The police marksmen surrounded the pen, rifles pointing at the boy crouched in the fork of the tree trunk.

Mel rushed over to the sergeant. 'Please, call your men off. Give Eve a chance!'

'Absolutely not. That creature is clearly out of control, probably rabid. On my mark . . .!' shouted Sergeant Bolter.

'Eve!' yelled Mel.

'Fire!'

But Eve was already moving. She leapt, plucked the boy from the tree, and covered him with her own body as the rifle bullets struck. The pair tumbled to the ground and lay still.

'Oh my stars!' moaned Sergeant Bolter. 'We've just shot Queen Victoria's favourite monster!'

Mel was so angry he wanted to kick the policeman but he held off, knowing they weren't finished here yet. 'Eve, are you all right?'

Eve stood up. Glaring at the policemen, she picked off the bullets that had flattened against her skin, which was fortunately tougher than rhino hide. 'That sergeant is very impolite.'

The boy on the ground sobbed and scuttled closer to her.

'*Mon petit?*' No response, so she repeated it much louder.

From within the folds of his cloak, the boy held out an apple. Eve took it from him with polite thanks. She threw it into the far corner so the howler monkeys would chase it and stop screaming their protests at her.

'I think we should go somewhere we can talk.' She lifted the boy up in her arms and leapt out of the cage, an amazing standing jump. She landed by Mel. Clutching at her, the boy in Eve's arms began a hurried tumble of an explanation but in a language Mel couldn't follow.

After allowing a little time for the conversation to unfold, the sergeant cleared his throat. 'Excuse me, madam, but can you tell me what it is saying – and more importantly, what is it? Another giant like yourself?'

Eve gave the man who had ordered her to be a shot a quelling look. Mel knew she did not think herself to be out of proportion – she considered the rest of the world to be rather short. 'He is just a boy – not more than fourteen, I would guess.'

'A boy? As big as that?' marvelled the sergeant.

'A large boy because he does heavy work,' conceded Eve. 'He is very difficult to understand. He speaks

French in such a way that I only comprehend it after much thought.'

'Does he have a name?' asked Mel, eyeing the shrouded figure curiously. His frame seemed oddly hunched over like he was cuddling something to his chest.

'Naturally. He says he is called Quasimodo le Petit.'

'The small? If that's small, I'd like to see Quasimodo le Grand,' said Mel.

Eve began walking back towards the bear enclosure. 'He wants his pretty fruit, he says.'

'And, madam, did he say how he got here?' asked the sergeant.

Eve shrugged. 'I really cannot understand what he says. It must be a dialect from another part of France.'

Returning to the bears, Mel took his first good look at the crate of fruit, Quasimodo's only possession. In the moonlight something glinted among the pineapples: something quite large and egg-shaped.

Eve put the boy down. 'Stay with Mel Foster. He is a good boy. He will look after you.' She then bent the bars of the enclosure, strode through the gap into the cage, careless of the watchful bears, picked up the crate and carried it out. Once she deposited it at Quasimodo's feet she straightened the bars and dusted off her hands.

Mel watched as Eve crouched before the huddled stranger, her black hair rippling down the back of her black uniform to touch the floor. She held out a hand, the slimmer of her two mismatched ones. Mel heard her say that Quasimodo needn't fear, they were friends; if he came with them he'd get something better to eat than fruit.

'*Vraiment*?' Really? asked the boy huskily.

'Come, *mon petit*,' Eve waggled her fingers. 'Mel Foster, we take him home.'

'Just a moment.' Mel still wanted a closer look at the shiny object he had spied. He moved a pineapple aside and scooped it out. 'What the Dickens!' In his palm lay a flawless gold egg. He flicked the catch holding the two halves of the shell closed and a little scene sprang into action: a miniature of a tall giantess made out of jet kicking a scrawny little silver man into a diamond river.

'*Joli oeuf!*' grunted the French boy, reaching out to take it from Mel. Too stunned to stop him, Mel let the Fabergé egg go. The boy hid it under the fold of his cloak but, unfortunately, not before the sergeant had seen it.

'Eve?' said Mel.

'*Oui?*'

'I think we have another problem.'

Eve was gently steering Quasimodo towards the gate. Having been in the ice for sixty years, she did not know the significance of the jewelled egg. 'Oh? What kind of problem?'

Quasimodo loped beside her, looking up with a dogged affection for his new friend.

'That kind,' said Mel, pointing at the policemen.

'Quasimodo Petit, or whatever your name is,' announced the sergeant. 'Monster, I'm arresting you on suspicion of theft – breaking and entering a royal palace . . .'

'And a zoo!' chipped in the keeper, still in a bad mood from having had his animals used as springboards. 'Disturbing the bears – not to mention what you did to that giraffe.'

'That too. You will accompany us to the station for further questioning.'

Quasimodo gazed at the two men with a quizzical expression in his grey eyes. His shock of scraggy brown hair flopped over his face, making him seem more bearlike than human.

'Sergeant, he doesn't understand,' pleaded Mel. 'Please, let him come with us. He's scared enough as it is!'

'But you saw it – you found it. He has the evidence on him. That's the Tsar's Fabergé egg he's clutching, or I'm the King of Spain. As for him, he doesn't need to understand to go to gaol. Men, arrest the monster!' The sergeant beckoned the other police officers forward with a flick of his truncheon.

Six armed police officers moved closer, two carrying heavy chains. With a sinking heart, Mel realized that they had intended to take Quasimodo prisoner from the start; Eve and he had been used to make him come quietly.

'But we promised him he'd be safe!' protested Mel as the police circled Quasimodo.

'What are they doing?' asked Eve, still too new to the ways of the modern world to understand the deception.

'Be reasonable, young sir,' said the sergeant. 'We were told to take him in for questioning as anyone breaking into impregnable buildings with fruit is under suspicion. No one knows how he got into the zoo.' He rubbed his chin. 'And he's got the egg.'

'But he's just a boy!' argued Mel.

'A boy that big? Ha! He's a monster. If you interfere, sir, then I'm afraid I'm going to have to arrest you too. Aiding and abetting a criminal.' The policeman gave Eve a wary look. 'Even if we have to shoot her again. I know my duty.'

Mel quickly thought through their options: with the queen so upset about the orange, the Monster Resistance couldn't count on support from the palace at this point. The police now knew where they lived so they couldn't make a dash for freedom and hide Quasimodo there, not without inviting a search down upon their heads and they had many more secrets that wanted preserving from the public eye.

'What do we do, Mel Foster?' asked Eve.

'We have to let them take Quasimodo for the moment,' said Mel reluctantly. 'Explain to him if you can. Promise that we will get him out. Having the stolen egg doesn't necessarily make him the thief.' Though

Mel had to admit that appearances were against Quasimodo's innocence.

A policeman approached Quasimodo with a set of handcuffs. Finally understanding their intent, the stranger began to wail.

'*Mam'selle!*' His friendly grey eyes turned bleak with the shock of betrayal.

'Don't take him!' shouted Eve, shoving one policeman off. He flew into a rubbish bin twenty feet away.

'Eve, you can't! You'll be arrested!' said Mel, grabbing her sleeve. 'We can't help Quasimodo if we're in prison too!'

'I have to let him go?' She looked quite white with fury.

'Yes, you have to let him go.'

'I hate this!' Eve released her hold on Quasimodo and the policemen swooped, wrestling him to the ground.

'*Aidez-moi!*' he called, but she had to turn away.

'*Menteuse!*' cried Quasimodo as the four policemen pulled him away towards their van.

'What did he say?' asked Mel.

'He called me a liar – and I did lie, didn't I? I said he'd be safe!' Eve was trembling with rage and shame. 'This is not right, Mel Foster!'

'No, it's not. We'll get him back, I promise.' Mel felt guilty he hadn't guessed the sergeant's intention from the start. He was wiser to the ways of the world than Eve, who tended to think the best of everyone. 'But we need answers if we are going to help Quasimodo. How he did get here and why did he have the egg? He said he thought it pretty, but that pretty thing is made of diamonds and belongs to the Tsar of Russia!'

'True. And why is *un bossu français* here in London in the first place?'

'What's a "bossu"?'

Eve searched her memory for the translation. 'A hunchback – one with the spine that curves, no?'

'The hunchback of Regent's Park – another mystery to add to the egg theft. Let's hurry back and see if anyone at home can guess the answers.'

Chapter Three

The Empire's Best Hunter

When Mel and Eve were allowed in to visit Quasimodo the next morning, they discovered him chained to the wall of his cell – a practice that was reserved for only the most dangerous criminals. The terrible part in Mel's view was that the boy did not protest the treatment. He seemed to expect to be chained up in a bare cell surrounded by hostile guards and jeering prisoners. He was sitting on the floor in the corner nursing a butterfly that had flown in through the barred window.

From the broken look of one wing, his new pet wasn't going to be flying out.

'Quasimodo?' called Eve softly. She then proceeded to tell him how sorry she was that he was in this fix, that they had not known what the police intended.

Quasimodo's answer was a shrug.

She began gently to question him about his origins and if there was anyone they could contact for him. Slowly, she coaxed replies out of him. While she did so, Mel had a chance to get a closer look at the stranger, better than he had managed in the moonlight of Regent's Park zoo. Quasimodo had long brown hair that badly needed a wash and comb. It had knotted into thick clumps like lots of little lambs' tails. His rags had been replaced with a prison uniform and showed that his shoulders were broad, arms strong, one foot slightly turned in as if he'd had an injury that had not healed properly. A star-shaped scar marred his left cheek. He frequently cupped his ears to block out sound that only he could hear, shaking his head in pain, giving grunts of distress. Quasimodo would not win any beauty contests, that was true, but his grey eyes were pleasant, their expression gentle, if a little confused. Mel seriously doubted Quasimodo would have the cunning to pull off the theft of which he stood accused.

'What does he say?' asked Mel when Eve paused to think over the answers to her questions.

'It is stranger than we thought. His father was the

one called Quasimodo le Grand but I'm not sure that he means his real father but rather one who looked after him. He says that all those born with the hunchback are outcast in his city. Only the cathedral of Notre Dame will give them shelter. Notre Dame was the closest thing he had to home in Paris.'

'Surely Paris isn't that bad?' wondered Mel.

'That is the odd part,' said Eve. 'I asked him to describe his home, thinking I had mistaken his meaning, and he describes a city of Gypsies and dancing bears, noblemen and priests, all living in the fear of a return of a terrible plague. Is Paris like that?'

'I don't think so. I think it's a bit like London but, well, French. And with better food.'

'It gets worse. The ignorant peasants of Paris recently drove his father to his death just because he was different and they feared him.' Eve scowled in disgust.

'How different?' asked Mel.

'He and his father were both born with crooked spines and had become a little deaf from ringing the bells. He says his people do not like those who are not perfect.'

Remembering how the monsters had been caged and persecuted under the Chief Butler a few months ago in London, Mel found he could believe that cruelty. 'That's so sad.'

'*Oui*, but I cannot understand everything he says therefore maybe I am missing something important.'

Eve wrinkled her brow, lines on one side distinctly higher than the other. 'His French is so peculiar. He uses words that I have only met with in old poetry. It is quite beautiful really. I think he reads my lips mostly as he can't hear me when I speak in a normal voice.'

Checking the guards weren't looking, Mel took his Monster Resistance diamond badge off his lapel. He pushed it through the bars. 'Tell him this is a gift from me.'

'Are you sure?' whispered Eve.

'Very.'

Quasimodo's eyes went immediately to the lapel pin. Carefully placing the butterfly to one side, he scooped the badge up between finger and thumb.

'It's yours. A present,' Eve assured him in French.

Tears filled the stranger's eyes and he cupped it in his palm. He turned it to the light to admire the gleams and flashes off the gems.

'*Merci*,' he whispered. '*Joli*.'

Wishing they could take him home with them, Mel waved at the prisoner. 'That's my promise that we'll be back. We promise.'

Mel and Eve returned home on the underground railway, feeling wretched about how they had left things. They had a whole carriage to themselves thanks to the fact that as soon as they got in all the other passengers, including the guard, decamped to another one. Mel shrugged: at least it gave them a private place

40

to talk with no risk of being overheard. As the steam train chugged through the tunnels, the smoke billowed and the darkness sparked with embers. It was a little like riding a dragon, complete with ear-piercing hoot.

'We have got to get him out of there, Mel Foster,' said Eve, scowling at her reflection in the windows.

'I know – but he looks guilty, doesn't he?'

'That boy would not know what he had done if it were him. He could have been used by someone to steal, yes, but to plan it himself, no. He is too . . .' she searched for a word, 'shy.'

Mel agreed with her but their plans to start immediately on a strategy to release Quasimodo were thwarted by finding a summons to the palace waiting for them on the hall table. Cracking the seal, Mel read it quickly. The Empire's best hunter had arrived and their presence, along with that of Lady Viorica Dracula, was required immediately (underlined twice) so their scents could be eliminated from the search. They were also to bring items belonging to the monster fairies and the twins.

'Lady Viorica, we've got to go out!' Mel called as Eve broke the bad news to the mummy who had just retired to his sarcophagus.

The vampire appeared from the kitchens, looking paler than usual, a cup of blood in hand. 'But I haven't slept.'

'Nor have we.' Mel waved the letter. 'The queen

needs us. Can you fetch some things belonging to the twins?' He started upstairs.

'Whatever for?' She abandoned her breakfast on the hall table and followed him.

'Sounds like they've brought in dogs,' speculated Mel as he grabbed a couple of the fairies' tiny boots from under his bed. Even in diminutive size, the footwear carried a hefty pong. 'The police have some specially trained bloodhounds. But that's not all that's going on. We'll fill you in on what happened last night on the way.'

On arrival at Buckingham Palace, however, there were no signs of bloodhounds or policemen. A scarlet-clad soldier in a bearskin helmet escorted Mel, Eve and Viorica through the plush corridors and up a flight of carpeted stairs to the throne room, site of the crime. All the participants in the award ceremony were represented either in person or through something that bore their scent. Mr Copperfield was sitting at a leather-topped desk, painstakingly tagging each one and checking their names off on a list. Mel had his tag hooked to his top buttonhole, Viorica and Eve were handed one to put on their wrist.

'Move along and join the others please, Master Foster,' said Mr Copperfield, raking his hair to stand up in peaks like whipped egg white. 'So many to get through!'

Seeing that their friend was harried by the task and

had no time for a chat, they took the same seats they had occupied at the ceremony. Mel put the fairy boots and the items belonging to the twins on their empty chairs.

'What do we do now?' he whispered.

'We wait.' Eve crossed her arms.

An awkward muttering filled the room from the other people attending in person. The chamber made an odd sight: chairs filled either by pale-faced guests or their representatives in the shape of gloves and hats. It was as though a wizard had gone through the room and transformed people at random into articles of clothing. Perhaps they should reconsider the magic theory Abel had rejected? Mel swung his legs as his feet didn't quite reach the ground. He bumped his heels together, making a pleasing clicking noise.

Viorica turned, blue eyes flashing with a glint of red. 'Do you have to do that?'

'Sorry. I'll whistle if you prefer.' He gave her a fake smile.

'You are a reckless boy, Mel Foster,' said Eve but Mel thought he saw her smile.

Suddenly, Viorica jumped to her feet and threw her arms wide. Mel felt a twist of alarm that he had pushed her too far and she was going to bite. He prepared to dive behind Eve. The vampire shimmered into a sparkling grey mist and shifted from her girl shape. The mist reformed, stretched, sprouting four paws, a snout

43

and whiskers. Her empty dress flopped to the floor and was shaken off the hind legs of a sleek grey wolf. The dowager duchess sitting next to Viorica gave a shriek and fainted into the arms of a frail elderly lord who promptly collapsed under her weight. The wolf ignored the consternation she had caused; she lifted her snout and howled.

'What's Viorica doing?' asked Mel, gripping Eve's forearm.

'I don't know – but listen.'

Deep in the bowels of Buckingham Palace, a chorus of wolf howls replied.

'Kingdom Brunel!' exclaimed Mel.

Viorica turned in an ecstatic circle, chasing her frond-like tail. The click of claws on polished floors could be heard coming ever closer. The double doors at the far end of the throne room burst open and four wolves bounded into the room. The humans screamed and retreated behind a barrier of swiftly arranged chairs – all except Mel and Eve. It took more than a wolf pack to scare them these days.

The wolves weren't the slightest bit interested in the people, however; they made straight for Viorica and gave her a good sniffing over before the three smaller ones began a friendly game of chase and nip. The largest wolf – a magnificent grey-coated male with a barrel-shaped white chest and keen amber eyes – stood watching with what Mel read as cool humour before raising his nose and giving a queer little run of yips and barks.

'Indeed, Grey Wolf, this is the strangest female wolf we have met.'

Mel jumped in surprise. A tall man had appeared at his shoulder so quietly Mel had no idea that he was there until he spoke right in his ear. Mel looked up – and up; the newcomer was dressed in a white knee-length tunic and baggy white trousers. He had long black hair, tied back with a band of trumpet-shaped flowers. Tanned a deep tea colour, his feet were bare in his worn leather sandals. Standing so close, Mel caught a whiff of the man's distinct scent: cardamom and wolf.

'Are you a werewolf, sir?' Mel asked. There were at least a score of werewolves now in London who had declared their true status so it wouldn't surprise him to discover another.

The man raised a thick black brow that arched over his honey coloured eyes. There was something wild in his gaze even in this refined setting. 'Werewolf? You think I'm a shape-shifter. I would enjoy that. No, I am wolf because I was raised by the pack.'

'Are these wolves yours, sir?' asked Mel.

The man threw back his head and gave a loud bark of laughter. 'No! They are my brethren. Grey Wolf and his brothers, Little Akela, Growler and Swift Bite. Brothers, come and be introduced.' He clapped his hands and the wolves broke off their play with Viorica to trot over, long pink tongues lolling, breath hot and sour. 'This must be Eve Frankenstein – I recognize her from the papers – and you are . . .?'

'Mel Foster,' said Mel quickly.

'Ah, another member of the Monster Resistance – we have heard of you even in the jungle. Hold out your hands so they can smell you.'

Mel thought he had probably done more sensible things than hold out his fingers within snapping distance of four wolves, one of whom was called Swift Bite. They gave him a quick sniff and spent longer over Eve's hands, presumably intrigued by the different scents coming from her patchwork body. Mel realized she probably carried the trace of all her original donors, a banquet for creatures that experienced the world largely through their noses.

'And who are you, sir?' Mel asked while the wolves were occupied by Eve.

The man opened his mouth to reply but a herald interrupted with a fanfare played on a silver trumpet.

'All stand for Her Imperial Majesty,' called Mr Copperfield.

Everyone, even the wolves, turned to face the little old lady in black, a diamond brooch glittering on her bodice. Queen Victoria took a seat on the red cushion waiting on the throne, placing her feet on the footstool. Two sombre ladies-in-waiting dressed in mourning clothes flanked her like Odin's ravens. One white hand draped on the arm of the gilded chair, Her Majesty lifted a finger.

'Approach, Forester Mowgli, best hunter in all India and the Empire,' cried the herald.

Mel was not much surprised when the man next to him stepped forward. Mowgli made his way to the foot of the dais, put his hands to his forehead and bowed. The wolves followed him, repeating the gesture as suited their species, with a dip of their snouts.

'Forester Mowgli, we thank you for coming so swiftly to our aid,' said the queen in her imperious high tones.

'It was fortunate that I was escorting tree specimens to Kew Gardens, Your Majesty,' replied Mowgli.

'Indeed – the only fortunate thing in this whole sorry affair. You understand your task?'

'Yes, Your Majesty: my brethren and I are to find the thief.'

'We have summoned all who were present at the ceremony so you may eliminate them from your hunt. You may start with me.' She held out a hand glittering with diamond rings. At a nod from Mowgli, the largest wolf crept forward and took a careful sniff of her fingertips. 'You have been told we have just taken a suspect into custody?'

'Yes, ma'am.'

'If you can find a trace of him in this room, that will provide the evidence linking him to this heinous theft as well as that in St Petersburg. Our police officers believe he is part of the conspiracy to steal the world's most valuable objects. They must be stopped.'

'We will do our best, Your Majesty.' Mowgli bowed again.

'Then we will leave you to your task. We expect everyone to cooperate with our imperial hunter to the fullest of their abilities.' Her little dark eyes swept the room, peer and porter alike. 'Disobedience will not be tolerated.' She stood up and bustled out, the two ladies-in-waiting hurrying after her.

'She's really got her state robes in a twist about this,' murmured Mel to Eve.

'I do not blame her.' Eve sat down on the nearest chair. It groaned under her weight but held. 'She must be thinking that if the thief can get in here without being seen, he can go anywhere. No secret is safe from him. Think of the papers he could steal from the government and sell to enemies – military plans and tactics, and that is just for a beginning.'

Mel fretted the tasselled fringe of the heavy curtain tie. He had to admit she had a point. He'd been thinking it all rather amusing up till now, but the consequences could be grave, even lead to war if the wrong information were spilled. Just a glance occasionally at the headlines in the newspapers told Mel that European powers were fiercely competitive and did not need much of an excuse to muster their armies.

While Mel and Eve had been talking, Mowgli and his brothers had made a thorough examination of the room. Viorica had slunk off with her dress in her jaws to transform somewhere privately. One by one the guests were sniffed and dismissed until only Mel, Eve and Mr Copperfield remained.

'Do you need us?' asked Mel, wondering why they hadn't been sent home.

'Copperfield sahib said you witnessed the theft,' said Mowgli squatting on the floor beside Mel.

'We don't know what we saw,' said Mel. 'A blur, nothing clear. What did you find out?'

'It is difficult to be certain in a room that has held so many people but we have smelt one very strange scent that does not belong to any of those on the guest list.'

Viorica returned to the chamber and took a seat next to Eve. The smallest wolf immediately curled up at her feet while two others leaned either side of her chair like bookends. Grey Wolf stretched out in the space between them all, a living hearthrug. Gingerly Mr Copperfield joined them, opting to stand next to Mel, the least alarming person in the room.

'Can you describe the scent, forester? Man or woman?' asked Mr Copperfield.

Mowgli scratched Grey Wolf's neck. 'A man. Not very clean.'

Mel's heart sank. It was not looking good for Quasimodo.

'Did you compare it to the rags the police brought to you this morning – those taken from the prisoner?' asked Mr Copperfield eagerly.

'Yes. Not that one. The cloth smelt of horse and smoke; the trace here is of someone who does not bathe – they are very different. We would not confuse the two.'

'Oh.' Mr Copperfield drooped at the news, having hoped for a rapid result to their investigation to please the queen.

'Then Quasimodo isn't the thief!' said Mel.

'No,' said Mowgli, 'he was not responsible for the theft. But he does carry a whiff of something that we also found in here – something we have not smelt before so I cannot name. Perhaps we should meet this Quasimodo?'

Mr Copperfield looked grimly at the pile of belongings he had to return to their owners and then at Mel. 'Master Foster, I would be most obliged if you would take care of the introductions. Indeed, if the Monster Resistance would work with Forester Mowgli and his . . . er . . . brothers, that would be the best solution for all of us.'

'They can stay with us,' said Viorica swiftly.

Mel felt a twinge of annoyance. Viorica was the most defensive of their home, fighting his presence there from the beginning on the grounds that he wasn't monster enough for them, but throw a few wolves into the mix and then suddenly she was Miss Society Hostess. It wasn't fair.

'Do you think the twins will agree?' asked Eve. They had strict rules about who was allowed inside: the first qualification was that you had to be a monster. Mel had got in on a technicality: the Chief Butler had put him on the Monster List so they had decided he qualified even before they were aware of his only unusual power, which was to blast things with his electric life force.

'A man raised as a wolf cub, wolves who act like his brothers: I say they will,' said Viorica firmly.

Mowgli gave her a wry smile. 'Let me ask my pack before we agree to leave our hotel and transfer to your territory.' He proceeded to explain the offer in a run of growls and yips. Grey Wolf rolled over on his back for a tummy rub, which appeared to be answer enough. 'They agree. Thank you. We were having trouble with the lift at the Savoy Hotel.'

'Oh, I'm very sorry. They usually give exemplary service – everything in tip-top condition. That's why I chose it for you,' said Mr Copperfield.

'It is not the lift that is at fault. It is that the boy who operates it. He flees every time we enter.'

'*Bien*,' said Eve, rising from her chair. 'That is settled. You will stay with us. Let us make haste to Newgate and see if you can cast any more light on the mystery.'

'And if you can prove Quasimodo innocent that would be wonderful,' Mel added. 'I don't like to think of him spending a minute more in gaol than he has to.'

'Innocent? That might not be possible. I am only a hunter in the Queen's Indian Forestry Service,' said Mowgli modestly.

Mel had returned to his usual state of mind, which was to be optimistic. 'Only the best hunter in all India and the Empire. If you can't find the real thief, then I don't know who can.'

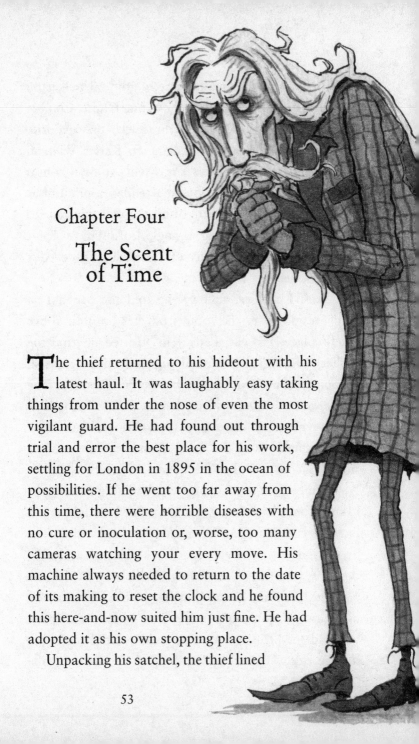

Chapter Four

The Scent of Time

The thief returned to his hideout with his latest haul. It was laughably easy taking things from under the nose of even the most vigilant guard. He had found out through trial and error the best place for his work, settling for London in 1895 in the ocean of possibilities. If he went too far away from this time, there were horrible diseases with no cure or inoculation or, worse, too many cameras watching your every move. His machine always needed to return to the date of its making to reset the clock and he found this here-and-now suited him just fine. He had adopted it as his own stopping place.

Unpacking his satchel, the thief lined

up his booty on the mantelpiece: a gold inkwell from President Cleveland's desk in the White House, Chinese Empress Dowager Cixi's jade bracelets, the favourite antique duelling pistols belonging to Kaiser Wilhelm of Germany, Japan's Emperor Meiji's oldest bonsai tree. This last had been lovingly tended for centuries by a specially trained cadre of monks. They fasted for six weeks before pruning a single leaf. With a grunt of pleasure, the thief broke off a branch and tucked it behind his ear.

'Aren't I a clever fellow?' he told the Mona Lisa who presided over the room from her position above the fireplace. His cat, Lady Jane, trotted in from the scullery where she had been dining on the prime Scottish salmon that he had left her before he went out. The tabby wound round his legs then leapt into her golden basket with velvet cushion in a warm nook by the fire.

The thief poked the embers and put on another shovel of coal to make Lady Jane comfortable.

'Shame about that Fabergé egg, isn't it, puss? Maybe I should have left Miss Mona alone but I thought you'd like the company.' As he tickled her under the chin, he thought over the epic journey he had made, going the long way round, travelling all the way in the one place he knew had changed little over the centuries, the cathedral of Notre Dame. But that stupid hunchback boy had tried to stop him and ended up coming along for the ride. That was when he had decided to make use of him. He would make the boy a scapegoat for his crimes, planting the jewelled egg on him. They had probably found the hunchback in the zoo by now. The lad was too foolish and ugly: no one would give him a chance to prove his innocence. With any luck, the police would decide they had their man and stop looking for the real thief. That would give him a chance to go back and nab the queen's brooch, the one containing the Koh-i-Noor diamond. That would look rather fine next to the gem he had taken from the crown. The third and largest in the set of diamonds in the Crown Jewels was in the sceptre but that object was kept in the Tower and harder to reach as the vault had always been guarded and it was only taken out once a year. He was still working out how to be on site to liberate that gem. If – maybe that should be when? – he got all three, he'd have them made into cufflinks perhaps? Or tie pins? No, fobs for his watch chain – that would be grand. He could just imagine Lady Jane chasing the sparkles across the room when he held them up to the light.

Pulling his Swiss pocket watch from his waistcoat, he checked the time. Seeing the hands were a little past midnight he nodded in satisfaction. He'd been away four minutes. Not bad for a round trip of some twenty-five thousand miles. A yawn bubbled up inside him, emerging in an onion-smelling burp. He'd taken it slowly but maybe that curry from the street vendor in India on the way back had been a mistake. Time to put up his feet and enjoy his collection. All this travelling was making him feel old.

He had barely settled into his favourite armchair by the fire when someone knocked on the door a floor below.

'Who do you think that is, Lady Jane, calling at this time of night?' Muttering curses to himself, the thief hauled his aching bones out of the seat and clambered down the steep staircase into the single room below that served as kitchen and sitting room for guests. They would be able to see his light and know that he was in; he had to behave as if all were normal inside his dwelling. He had chosen his hideout as it was the last place anyone would expect to find a haul of treasures so he had little fear that the law had caught up with him. Probably some annoying urchins collecting for Guy Fawkes Night. Making sure there was no sign of his riches, that the door at the top of the stairs was firmly closed, he pulled a scraggy dressing gown over his velvet suit, tugged a mildewed old nightcap over his wispy grey hair, then opened the front door.

'Why are you disturbing an old man at his poor supper?' he grumbled. 'Can't a body get a moment's peace?' In fact he had a nice glass of claret waiting and a T-bone steak on the hotplate above, but his caller wasn't to know that.

There were no children with a stuffed dummy begging for pennies. A man in a dark opera cloak with the collar turned up stood on the step, his back to the door. The first chill of fear ran through the thief. Maybe he should have brought one of the duelling pistols with him? Slowly the gentleman turned. He had a wide brimmed top hat pulled low over his eyes so his face was in shadow.

'Krook?'

The thief nodded automatically before he realized what he had done. No one knew his real name in this decade. 'I mean, no. Don't know anyone of that name – never have, never will! I'm Mr Smith, me.' He made to close the door but the man shoved an ebony walking cane in the hinge.

'Don't be foolish: I know exactly who you are, what you have done, and how you are doing it.'

Krook's heart pounded, sounding in his ears like the horses' hooves on Derby Day, but he wasn't going to admit anything. 'Bully for you. Run along or I'll call the police!'

'I doubt that very much. You have more to hide than I do.' A glint of white teeth shone in the light spilling from Krook's kitchen fire. 'You had better ask me in.'

That was the absolute last item on the list of things Krook wanted to do. 'Sorry but I'm busy. I've got . . . got the plague.' He started coughing and spluttering.

The man shook out a snowy handkerchief and held it to his mouth. A black half-mask hid his eyes. The effect was more highwayman than opera-goer, but definitely still a gentleman. 'I suppose that is possible, but I'll take my chances inside. I prefer that we conduct our business in private.' He pushed past the old man. Once inside, he used his cane to tap the door closed. Krook could do nothing but gape. Somehow this confident gentleman had taken over and Krook wasn't sure how the visitor had done it or why he had let him.

'I'm sure you have somewhere more comfortable to discuss my proposition than this.' Dismissing the grey walls and threadbare carpet that smelt of cat, the man tried a few doors leading to the scullery and cupboards, before taking the stairs to the sitting room where the Mona Lisa hung. 'Very astute of you to choose this place.' He put his top hat on a marble bust of Julius Caesar. 'That was the hardest part – finding out where you live in 1895.' Slipping the chain that held his cloak at his neck, the gentleman discarded the red-satin-lined cloak on to the sofa. It lay like a pool of blood against the canary yellow upholstery. Keeping his cane and mask, he sat in Krook's chair. 'I'll have a glass of the same.' He nodded at the claret.

With a shaking hand, Krook poured a second drink, spilling a few drops on an original Leonardo da Vinci drawing of a flying machine.

'Tsk, tsk!' The man wiped them off with a waft of the handkerchief. 'If you are going to go to so much trouble to take it, you really should look after it.'

Krook found some of his bravado returning. What

58

did the man really know about him? Just that he handled stolen goods. Give him a few seconds on his own and he and Lady Jane could be far, far away from here.

The gentleman stroked the side of his glass with a black-gloved finger. Krook noted the strong throat peeking out of the collar of his pristine shirt, high cheekbones, olive-toned skin and closely cut black hair – this was a thoroughbred rotter he was dealing with, no ordinary thug.

'I expect you are considering using your time machine to escape me?' said the man.

'What! No!' Krook took a step to stand between his unwanted visitor and his under-stairs cupboard. 'I don't have no time machine. You must be fit for Bedlam to say that!'

'Far from it. I suspect I'm the only sane person on this earth, certainly the cleverest. I know full well you are the unworthy recipient of one of my colleague's demonstration pieces. I was at a gathering in his house when he sent it off – into the future or the past he admitted that he did not know. I've been waiting for it to come back for many years now. When I learned of the three thefts last week, I realized that only a person with a time machine could have done it. I suppose you have been researching your targets, finding a point in history where the room was unguarded or perhaps not even there any longer, then sent yourself forward or back to the micro-moment you wanted to make the snatch? You come and go so quickly you're barely there at all. The fact that you haven't unwittingly ended up entombed in a wall shows that you have some skill with the device.'

Krook didn't like this, didn't like this at all. Best not to make any admissions or denials.

'You don't need to worry that I'm here on the Time Traveller's behalf to demand the return of his device. Oh no, he is far too interested in pure science to understand the potential of such a machine.'

'Potential?' Krook croaked despite himself.

The visitor waved a hand to the valuables around him. 'You've been collecting like a magpie – no strategy but what glitters and appeals to your greed. You do not realize that you've been handed a chance to turn the machine into the ultimate weapon.'

Krook didn't like weapons. He knew he couldn't shoot straight thanks to his short-sightedness and had no hope of wielding a sword. Stealing a few comforts was enough for him. 'You aren't making sense. You can't fight with that thing.'

The gentleman smiled slyly, acknowledging Krook's accidental admission that he had the machine. 'Really? I think your imagination is at fault. I can think of manifold ways to fight with it. Under my guidance, used rightly, that time machine can be turned into power.'

'What does a man like me want with that?'

The visitor continued to smile but it was a cold

expression, like the unintended grin in the setting of a shark's jaw. 'For a start you could stop hiding in a rat-infested slum of condemned houses and live openly in a mansion surrounded by your gains.'

'But it's convenient – unoccupied for years – by the river.'

'And smells like it. Why on earth live here when you could live in comfort and have pretty young servants to wait on you? Nobles who scorned you would bow before you.'

Krook had to admit it was a nice enough image. When he had been landlord of his rag and bottle shop, he had had to bow and scrape to all the gentry. 'What would I have to do? Not that I'm saying I'll do anything, mind.'

'You could begin by holding the whole country to ransom. Just think: a few carefully picked targets, you swoop in and remove them beyond saving and demand a ransom for their safe return.'

'You mean, *harm* people? No, I don't do that.'

The gentleman admired the shine of his ruby-red drink in the firelight. 'You've already taken one boy from medieval Paris, I can't see that you have any right to pretend you are squeamish.'

'That was a mistake. I'm never going back so far again – I almost got lynched as a warlock! Anyway, he's a hunchback – a monster.' Krook felt he had to make his position clear. 'He shouldn't exist in the first place.'

The gentleman gave a shrug. 'So we start with the monsters: it will make your point clear enough to get the government worrying what you'll do next. I've picked an example you should be able to handle, the one called Melchizedek Foster. A puny specimen, hardly a monster at all. You take him somewhere out of the way and I'll handle the rest.'

Krook whipped off his nightcap. 'Hang on a minute: I haven't agreed to anything.'

With steely control, the visitor raised his cane and knocked a Ming vase off a side table. It shattered into hundreds of pieces. 'Oh dear. How clumsy of me.' He raised his cane again, aiming for a Venetian glass candlestick. It fell with a crack and two branches snapped off. Krook whimpered. The cane then moved round to Lady Jane's ornate cat basket where she was curled up asleep. It hovered like a snooker cue being lined up to take a potshot at her head.

'Please, don't hurt her!' moaned Krook.

'I've made my point, I trust? You now work for, and take your orders from, me – no one else.' The door opened again, letting in two men who were built for the boxing ring rather than a drawing room. 'Ah, and here are my associates. They'll be here in your charming house to ensure that you do what you are told. You will lose everything you hold dear if you dare disobey or try to run away. Have I made myself clear?'

Krook could just imagine what his existence would

become in thrall to this merciless man. 'Look, please, just take it.' He rushed over to the cupboard and hauled out the carriage-clock-sized device he had strapped to a broomstick.

'A time broom: how quaint,' said the gentleman, genuinely amused. 'But I don't want it. I'm not risking myself or any of my men when you are perfectly capable of doing the job.' He leaned over and rubbed the cat under the chin. Not knowing her peril, Lady Jane purred in her sleep and twisted, revealing her vulnerable white belly. 'We have an agreement?'

Numbly, Krook nodded. He had two things he loved in his life – himself and his cat – and this man was obviously a threat to both. He had to agree until he could think of a way out.

'Oh, and you can carry on with the fruit. Not my style but it has become your calling card.' The gentleman refastened the cloak at his throat. 'Watch that cat,' he added to his men.

'Who are you?' whispered Krook, wishing he could turn back time and not open the door. The problem was that the time paradox meant that Lady Jane would still be at risk. Krook couldn't interfere with his own timeline; he'd tried and his old self had just not seen him or reacted. He was a ghost to himself. That was why he always had to time things so he came back a few minutes after he left no matter how long or short the journey: he had to avoid crossing with himself.

The gentleman paused, swinging his cane nonchalantly. 'Did I not say? You can call me the Inventor.' He put his hat back on with a hollow tap to the crown. 'Good evening. Do make my men comfortable. It will be better for all concerned.' With a harsh tweak of the cat's tail, the Inventor left the room before she had time to swipe at him with her claws.

Mel sat cross-legged on the top of the Jekylls' carriage, which had been hauled into the courtyard to make more room for the wolves in the stables at the back of the house. He had a good view of the three youngest members of the pack, who were currently gambolling around the mummy, snapping at the trailing ends of his bandages as he tried to go about his business of peeling carrots for supper. If they carried on, they'd have him toppling into the little fountain in the middle of the cobblestoned yard – in fact, that was probably their aim. Mel had already fished him out a couple of times. Inky and Nightie had taken refuge in the fountain, clambering on to the top of the waterspout and putting their thumbs over the jet to deter any interested sniffing from one of their unruly visitors. Mel wished Eve was here but she had gone to spend some time with Quasimodo. She was teaching him English so he could communicate with his gaolers.

'Hey, wolves, stop teasing the mummy!' Mel called.

The wolves took no notice.

Faced with a more violent attack on one bandage, the mummy backed away from Growler and fell over Little Akela who had crouched behind him for just this result. Once on his back, the pack surrounded the mummy and began sniffing and nipping at his flailing limbs. Inky tried driving them off with water but the arc did not reach far enough and just wetted the stones instead.

'Stop it! Stop it!' squawked Nightie, beating the fountain bowl in frustration. 'He doesn't like that!'

Enough was enough. Mel had tried being nice for seven days now but who knew how much a reanimated mummy could put up with before real damage was done to his ancient bandages? Mel jumped down and strode over to the nearest of the wolves. 'I warned you!' Time to see if his target practice with his electricity would pay off. Drawing deep on his power, he reached for it and let a spark run down his arm to his fingers. He released it against Little Akela's haunch. It would feel like a stinging slap. The wolf yelped and turned but Mel was ready with a second spark, which got Little Akela on the snout. The youngster turned tail and fled into the stable. 'Do you want the same?' he threatened Swift Bite who had his teeth in the mummy's leg. Guilty brown eyes looked back at him. Mel threw a spark at the wolf's flank. Detaching himself from the Egyptian, Swift Bite slunk away, making a show of limping even though Mel knew he hadn't hit him that hard. 'Growler?' The last wolf decided he did not need a lesson. He let go quickly and trotted off, wagging his tail innocently.

Mel helped the mummy to his feet and rewound the bandages, tucking them back in the correct places. 'We are going to have to give serious thought to safety pins, my friend,' Mel muttered. 'And whose bright idea was it to invite those mutts home anyway?'

The mummy held his arms out in a 'what can you do?' gesture and headed for the relative safety of his kitchen.

The pack had moved in last week and since then had made life at the Jekylls' house very interesting in all the unpleasant senses of that word. The monster fairies had spoiled at least three of their favourite fancy dresses running away from the rough play of the young wolves; Mel had gathered more scrapes and bumps than he had as a cabin boy; and Jacob Marley was reduced to just plaintive moaning as he gazed on the damage done to the carpets in the downstairs rooms. Their leader, Grey Wolf, had done nothing to curb the behaviour of his three brethren, even joining in on occasion. Mowgli had explained that the wolves were being quite restrained for a wild pack. The forester had the annoying habit of replying to any complaints that this was all meant in fun and a sign that the wolves felt at home.

'I'd prefer them to feel a bit more like strangers then,' Mel had said.

Mowgli had just laughed, though Mel had not meant it as a joke.

At least Mowgli knew how to behave indoors, even if some of his habits were unorthodox. He had taken over the guest bedroom and rigged up a hammock rather than use the soft mattress. It was how he slept in the jungle, the forester explained.

'And when I lie on a bed, I feel like it is eating me,' Mowgli said, swinging to and fro in his canvas hammock.

The only person who was happy about the invasion of wolves was Viorica. She spent most of the time in wolf shape curled up with the rest of the pack. Mel did find some sympathy for her: being a vampire was a lonely business in the human world as most people were afraid she was going to bite them; at least biting seemed normal in the wolf kingdom and they accepted her as one of their own.

As Mel was trying to coax the fairies that it was safe to leave the fountain, the gate giving on to the mews behind the house crashed open and one of the twins strode through, shouldering a heavy trunk with ease. Hurrying over to check the eye colour – Cain's green irises were a shade lighter than Abel's – Mel offered help with the burden as the other twin paid off the hansom cab driver in the alleyway.

'Master Abel, how was the journey?' asked Mel, helping Abel in the muscular brother form dump the trunk on the cobbles. His glum spirits lifted. With the Jekylls back, they could help with the campaign to free Quasimodo who was still in Newgate.

'Vile. Cain was seasick.'

A light tap-tap of a cane heralded Cain's arrival. 'I was not – or only when in that body.' He prodded his brother.

'Get off!'

Cain smiled. 'We've made the unfortunate discovery that our larger form is a very poor sailor.' He twirled his cane. 'I picked this up in St Petersburg – a cane for Cain – do you like it, Mel?'

'You've been all the way to Russia?' marvelled Mel.

'I think you look an idiot. I won't be carrying that thing when we swap,' muttered Abel.

'You'll have to if I make it our signature piece when out in society,' returned Cain.

'Then that cane will suddenly find itself in many pieces, some of which will be shoved up your . . .'

'What did you discover at the palace and in the Louvre?' Mel asked quickly. Clearly two weeks in each other's company, much of which had been spent feeling seasick, had strained the twins' relationship.

'Two mysteries to match the one at Buckingham Palace,' replied Cain. 'We've brought some evidence home with us for our guests to examine. Thank you for your telegrams by the way.' He gazed round the courtyard for their guests. 'A man raised by wolves sounds most intriguing. We're looking forward to meeting him.'

'You won't be thinking that for long,' muttered Mel. So the twins had just accepted the newcomers like everyone else, had they? He was hoping they would at least put up a protest as they had before allowing him join the Resistance.

'Get him for us, will you?' said Abel. 'Inky, can you ask the mummy to rustle up a cuppa for a weary traveller?' He sat down on the edge of the fountain and examined the shivering fairies. 'What you two doing in there?'

'Safest place,' squeaked Nightie, hugging Inky for warmth.

'Bad doggies!' elaborated Inky, holding out the ragged end of his once fine yellow dress.

'What? The wolves? You just have to show them who's boss.'

Mel gave a cough to disguise his laughter. 'Yes, like that is going to work.'

Abel scowled. 'Just fetch our guest, would you?'

'If you want him, you only have to do this.' Mel put two fingers in his mouth and let out a swooping whistle. The wolves in the stable howled in reply. 'Mowgli has excellent hearing.'

A window upstairs was thrown open and a dark head poked out. 'What do you require, Mel?'

'The twins have returned. They want to meet you.'

Mowgli turned and made a series of yips and growls to an unseen Grey Wolf.

'He speaks wolf?' asked Cain, getting out his notebook from his breast pocket. 'Has anyone tried to record the language?'

Abel flicked water at him. 'Focus, brother: evidence first.'

Cain sighed. 'Ah yes. I'm obliged to you for the reminder.'

The upper window was shoved up higher and Mowgli climbed out on to the ledge.

'There are stairs, you know!' called Mel, used now to the bizarre ways that Mowgli had for getting about the house.

With a flash of a grin, Mowgli leapt to the drainpipe and slid down.

'Newton's wig: that's extraordinary,' muttered Cain, fingers tightening around the little pencil attached to his notebook. 'He moves like a squirrel through the forest canopy.'

'He says he's never lived in a house with more than one floor, unless you count a tree house,' explained Mel.

Mowgli crossed the courtyard and bowed.

Cain held out his hand. 'It's an honour to meet you, sir.'

Mowgli looked at the hand for a second then took it gingerly in his, letting Cain shake his arm up and down without joining in the gesture – another part of London life Mowgli had not experience before, Mel guessed.

'All right, mate?' asked Abel, tapping his forehead in a cockney greeting.

'Yes, I "all right",' replied Mowgli carefully. 'Are you all right too, mate sahib?'

'I'm afraid my brother is still feeling the effects of our sea voyage,' said Cain, 'otherwise he would rise to greet you.'

'You should chew on ginger,' Mowgli suggested. 'That's what I did on the passage from India.'

'I'll try that. Thanks,' said Abel.

'Thank you, sahib, for your hospitality. Not many houses welcome wolves.' Mowgli's eyes went to the trunk. 'You have something for us?'

Cain flicked the catches and levered up the lid. 'We persuaded the authorities to give us objects from the rooms where the thefts were committed, things we can be fairly sure the thief touched. I'm afraid some of it hasn't travelled very well.' He pulled out a plank with a blackened banana skin still nailed to it; the fleshy part had gone.

Mowgli waved that objection away. 'No matter: we are used to following old trails. I'll summon my brethren.' He gave a harsh bark. The three young wolves padded out of the stable. Seeing the two newcomers by the fountain, they began their usual gambol and sniff act, daring even to tug at the laces on Abel's sturdy boots.

71

Abel clapped his hands under the nose of the offender. 'No.' He held up a hand, two fingers pointing towards Growler. 'You will behave.'

Growler looked at the fingers, then at Abel's cool green eyes. His tail drooped then began to swish placatingly, his head hung.

'Ah, I see you are an alpha,' said Mowgli approvingly.

Cain stroked the head of the nearest wolf, Little Akela, who was leaning submissively against his knee now. 'I think you'll find we both are, forester.'

Great, thought Mel. He'd had a week of problems only to discover what he should have been doing all along was give the pests a stern look and pat. He tried it on Swift Bite who was sniffing the ground at his feet. Swift Bite gave Mel a disdainful look in return and butted him in the stomach.

Mowgli pulled Swift Bite away. 'You're not an alpha. 'They regard you as one of the pack to be played with.'

Grey Wolf trotted out of the kitchen, ham bone clamped in his jaws, the mummy following behind, shaking his fist.

'What were we having for supper again?' said Mel. 'Oh yes: honey-roasted ham.'

Cain chuckled. 'I see that things have got a little out of control in our absence.'

'We've been thrown to the wolves, I think you'll find.'

'No matter,' said Abel, 'you can go and get another joint from the butchers in a moment.'

Mel sighed. He didn't want to be just a messenger boy in the Resistance.

'Let's see what the pack makes of our findings, brother. Mowgli sahib, if you would?'

Mowgli looked a little taken aback to hear a young gentleman addressing him so respectfully but Abel just carried on smiling, clearly meaning no mockery by it. 'This was from the Paris theft?' he asked, gesturing to the plank and fruit picture.

'Indeed. And this is from the Tsar's palace.' Cain drew out a heavy cream curtain wrapped round a pineapple.

Mowgli gave his brethren some instructions then stood back as they each took turns to sniff the items. While they were doing that, Mel retrieved the monster fairies and dried them off with the end of his shirt. Finished with the objects, the wolves settled down on their haunches in a circle and began a discussion carried out in twitches of ears, brows, yips and the occasional howl. Mowgli joined in, holding his hands up to his own ears to make up for his lack of moveable ones. Finally, he dropped his hands.

'It is the same as at the palace,' he said. 'There is the smell of an unwashed old man clinging to all these items – the same man in each case.'

'But that makes no sense,' said Cain, tapping his cane on the cobbles. 'The thefts were carried out at the same time; it can't be the same person.'

Mowgli waved a graceful hand, brushing aside the argument. 'There is more, something we do not understand, a scent that we've only ever discovered at these three places and clinging to that hunchback boy in your prison.'

'Interesting. What's that?' asked Abel.

'It is very hard to describe – like the abandoned cities that you find in the jungle.' Mowgli frowned. 'But not quite that. It smells like . . . like things from the past, present and future all in one perfume.'

'The scent of time?' Mel gazed at the rotting banana skin, the prickly pineapple and then recalled the blurred memory he and Eve had of the theft at the palace. 'You mean our thief can be in three places at once because he travels in time? That would be amazing!'

'But that's impossible,' said Abel.

'No, brother, just very, very unlikely.' Cain nudged the pineapple with his toecap. 'And it makes him exceedingly difficult to catch because he can dip in and out of our era, flitting out of reach any time we get close.'

'Can you track a thief through time?' Mel asked Mowgli.

The forester went very still, becoming a creature lurking in the jungle, stalking prey. 'No, but we can pick up the crossing of trails whenever they touch us. It would be like coming upon a path that we can't follow forward or back, but at least it would tell us someone had passed through.'

'Then we have our next step decided,' said Cain. 'Mowgli sahib, I'd be obliged if you would start the search.'

'But where, sahib?'

'Ah, that's the easy part,' said Abel. 'Just go anywhere there's stuff to steal.'

'I'd start with the Tower of London, if I were you,' added Cain. 'Abel and I had better look into time travel while you do it. Clearly someone has made great advances in this field while we weren't paying attention.'

'Unless they've come from the future,' added Mel. 'What's impossible now might be possible then.'

Cain acknowledged this with a nod. 'Ah, true. A good thought, Mel. So many paradoxes – we are in for a bumpy ride, my friends.'

Chapter Five

Not Really
a Monster

In the busy foyer of Scotland Yard, Sergeant Bolter looked in disbelief at the piece of paper Mel had handed him. 'I'm to release him?'

'Yes, officer.'

A man was dragged past, a string of knotted silk handkerchiefs dangling from his pocket like a polka dot tail. 'It weren't me, guv!' he protested.

'Noah, you're getting too old for this lark. Didn't the Dodger tell you to retire years back?' replied the arresting officer as he towed the pickpocket to the cells by the scruff of his neck.

Bolter was so used to the goings on in his police station that the shouting did not distract him. 'That hunchback is to be let go and handed over to you? You, a boy?'

Mel turned his attention back to the task in hand. 'Actually, I think you'll find I'm registered at Buckingham Palace as an authorized monster.'

'What makes you a monster then? No, don't tell me: I don't want to know.' The policeman cast a nervous look at Eve who was waiting patiently a few paces away from the reception desk, studying the pictures of various Wanted People tacked to the noticeboard. Even the most hardened villains and seasoned coppers were steering clear of her as they crossed the foyer. 'With the giantess, I can guess; but you – you could do something really horrible, like turn inside out, or . . . or grow three heads. With tentacles instead of teeth.'

Mel gave the officer points for having a particularly lurid imagination. 'I might.'

Sergeant Bolter rang the bell on the desk. Constable Wilkins, last seen holding the horses outside the zoo, popped his head out from the station's telegraph office. Mel could just see the lady operators tapping out their messages; the room sounded like it played host to a flock of frenetic woodpeckers.

'Wilkins, accompany these two young . . . persons to Newgate and release the monster we have in cell twenty-three to their custody. He's been granted bail.'

Wilkins saluted perkily. 'Righto, sarge.'

Then Sergeant Bolter bolted for safety, leaving them with the constable.

'You taking that monster boy home with you?'

Wilkins grabbed his helmet from a peg by the door. 'He'll like that, poor blighter. Didn't sit right with me: banging him up in gaol like that without even a hearing.'

'It was very wrong,' said Eve. 'It is fortunate that the queen herself has ordered that Quasimodo be granted bail.'

'How come?' asked Wilkins. 'I thought he was caught red-handed with the egg.'

'She has agreed that her best hunter has found evidence that someone else did the actual thieving,' explained Mel. 'He's not been cleared but that was good enough to let him out for the moment.'

'So there's another villain to catch, is there?' Wilkins hooked his thumbs in his wide black belt and sauntered out of the station. 'Smashing.' Reaching the pavement, he stopped, looking up and down the empty street. 'Can't see a cab. How do you want to get to the gaol? Underground?'

'No need: we've brought our own transport.' Mel gave a whistle and the mummy pulled out from the side street where he had been parked.

'Oh my Aunt Ethel's bloomers: that's just the most topping thing I've ever seen!' Wilkins did a little jig on the spot, police whistle dancing, truncheon hopping. 'Can he even see through those bandages?'

Mel liked the constable all the more for being more impressed by the mummy than the motorcar. 'I've never worked it out. Doesn't stop him though.'

Wilkins opened the passenger door and bowed to Eve. 'Mam'selle, after you.'

'*Merci*.' Lifting her skirt like the most refined of ladies, Eve slid into the front seat, her eyes lingering a little longer than usual on the flushed cheeks of the young police officer. The suspension groaned. Mel and Wilkins climbed in the back. The mummy held out his arm to indicate he was pulling out and eased the vehicle into the carriageway.

Just then a cab driver turned out on to Whitehall and made the poor decision of cutting up the motorcar. Outraged, the mummy squeezed the brass horn and gave six burping hoots accompanied with some very crude hand gestures. The cab driver now got a good look at the people in the front seats of the vehicle he had inconvenienced. He paled and pulled the hansom cab over to the side of the road to allow the motorcar to pass. Smugly, the mummy drove on with a final toot of the horn.

'Oh, your driver is a splendid chap! Do you think he'd let me have a go of his horn?' asked Wilkins as the mummy joined the traffic heading for Trafalgar Square.

'He might.'

The mummy detached the horn from the dashboard and tossed it to the rear seat. Wilkins caught it with a whoop and spent the journey accompanying the Egyptian's driving with a salvo of toots and brass burps.

Seeing that the other two were occupied with

terrorizing other drivers, Eve turned in her seat to talk to Mel. 'I like him – I like him very much. I think the mummy has found, how do you say, a spiritual brother?'

Mel chuckled. 'It's nice that the mummy's making friends outside the house. He's not had one of those for four thousand years.'

But their good mood drained away as the motorcar pulled up outside Newgate. The high walls of the prison had stood there so long that the stones had absorbed the misery and despair of those who had been incarcerated inside.

'What a horrible place! Let's get Quasimodo out of there,' said Mel, jumping down to the pavement.

Wilkins put his helmet on and straightened his uniform. 'Don't worry, young monster, sir, we'll have your French fruit boy out lickety split. Follow me.'

Eve sighed in appreciation.

With the constable's escort, Eve and Mel were allowed into the prison; but, as members of the public, they weren't allowed to fetch Quasimodo themselves. Normally a released prisoner would be brought to the people taking him home but in this case no one was willing to enter the cell to release the chains.

'We just don't know what he'll do, miss,' admitted the warden. 'We could send to the zoo for a neck loop, I suppose. Drag him out that way.'

Wilkins soon put an end to that idea.

'Blimey, you lot are a bunch of cowardly custards!

Give me the key. I'll fetch him.'

The warden slapped a thick iron key ring in Wilkins's hand. 'Good luck, constable. I'll tell your mother you died in the service of your country.'

'Preposterous!' muttered Eve.

With a jaunty salute, Wilkins walked off to stairs leading to the cells, braver at nineteen than all the old hands of thirty and forty.

'He likes shiny things!' Mel called out after him. He turned to Eve and asked in a low voice so the warden couldn't eavesdrop 'Quasimodo won't hurt Wilkins, will he?'

Eve shook her head. 'Not on purpose.'

It took a long while – long enough for Mel to start imagining the worst – but then Wilkins returned leading Quasimodo. His police whistle had relocated to round the boy's neck and Quasimodo was peeping on it merrily.

'Thanks for the tip about shiny things,' said Wilkins, looking a bit ruffled. There were a couple of new rips in his jacket. 'He didn't want to come at first but we reached an understanding. Just let him know he can't blow that thing out on the street or he'll have officers descending on him – and that he really wouldn't like. I have the feeling he don't much care for our uniforms.'

The constable really should have been a lion tamer, decided Mel. Even an angry boy of Quasimodo's dimensions, who had put up a fight before agreeing to come, had not jolted Wilkins from his cheerful stride.

'Thanks, Constable Wilkins. Can we give you a lift back?' asked Mel.

Eve fluttered her eyelashes coyly at the young policeman, an odd look as they weren't quite in unison. 'Would you care to have tea with us?'

'Oh yes, please!' Wilkins signed the release papers for the frowning warden. Fortunately he had missed the eye-fluttering. 'My shift is over now so I'd like nothing better.'

Mel tugged Eve's sleeve. 'Is that a good idea? We've got wolves staying, remember?'

Eve smiled softly. 'I think Constable Wilkins will manage admirably.'

Oh dear, Mel suspected Eve might be a bit sweet on Wilkins. Mel was about to warn her that she shouldn't develop a tender regard for the policeman but caught himself in time. Why shouldn't Eve fall in love? She was a young lady as well as an unusual creation, with her own hopes and dreams. If any ordinary person was going to appreciate Eve's unique qualities, it might be Wilkins.

Quasimodo had transferred his trust to Wilkins since the policeman was the one who had released him, so followed him obediently out to the motorcar. The French boy showed no surprise being ushered into a vehicle driven by a mummy but perhaps the last few days had been so extraordinary he had reached the point where nothing could shock. He sat between Mel and Wilkins watching the carriages and people pass outside, eyes flicking from object to object with a puzzled expression. He then turned to Mel and poked him with a forefinger.

'You Mel.'

'You speak English now?' Quasimodo was watching his lips so Mel made the effort to speak up, remembering the boy suffered from partial deafness. 'That's wonderful!'

'Eve teached me.'

Mel smiled. 'Yes, I'm Mel, Mel Foster.'

'Me, Quasimodo.'

'I know. Pleased to meet you.'

'You give badge.' Quasimodo held up his thumb to display the diamond lapel pin. 'Why?'

'Because you like pretty things.'

Quasimodo thought about this for a moment, then nodded. 'Thank you.'

Wilkins leaned forward so he could speak across the large boy sitting between them. 'He's not really a monster, is he? He's just a big lad with a back problem.'

Mel had often wondered about this. What made a monster? 'I'm not sure I know what a monster is. I'm quite happy to be one, so maybe he will be too.'

'My sergeant would say that monsters were something horrible, something scary, but I say that monsters are grand.' Wilkins patted Quasimodo's hand where it rested on a grubby knee. 'Look how you lot saved us from the Demon Butler. I'd like to be one. So much more interesting than being me.'

The motorcar turned into the mews behind the Jekylls' house. 'Hold that thought about interesting because you are about to meet quite a few more of us. Eve, can you keep the wolves away from our guests if they're back?' Mel found he was less worried for Wilkins than for Quasimodo. The last thing the newly released prisoner needed was to be mobbed by the over-enthusiastic pack.

Cain came out into the courtyard to greet the motorcar. In the rough brother body, he stood shoulder to shoulder with Quasimodo. 'Welcome to the Monster Resistance.' He clapped Quasimodo on the shoulder. 'We've a few questions for you but let's have some grub first, eh?'

Quasimodo shied away. 'Grub?' His eyes went to Wilkins for reassurance. 'What is that?'

'Food,' said Wilkins.

'*Nourriture, mon ami.*' Cain realized that Eve and Mel were intending to bring the policeman in with them. 'Are you two mad? You can't invite the law in here.'

Wilkins saluted Cain. 'Pleased to meet you, sir.'

'It is all right: he is my friend,' said Eve. 'He already knows where we live and he was the one who got Quasimodo out of his cell. Without him we might still be trying to persuade the warden to let him go.'

'Abel won't like this.' Cain suddenly grinned. 'But then Abel is still out with Mowgli and the wolves at the Tower of London. What he don't know won't hurt him.'

Mel trailed the four of them into the house, finding himself wondering if it had been just him they hadn't wanted, as everyone else who turned up appeared to get red carpet treatment.

The tea party was a huge success. Wilkins was charmed by all the monster inhabitants, even bold enough to pick up the imp who lived on a shelf in the pantry sealed inside a blue glass bottle. No one dared release it as it would sell your soul to the devil if you did so. The imp wasn't too pleased to be shaken about by the curious policeman, holding on to the sides of its bottle with tiny hands and spitting sparks that stopped at the glass.

'Oh, you lot are so lucky, living here,' sighed Wilkins, hand resting on the sleeping form of the mummy cat, who had settled in his lap. 'If you ever need a security guard, I'm your man.'

Cain offered him a plate of chocolate cakes baked in the shape of dung beetles. 'Thanks, Fred.' Wilkins was now on first-name terms with everyone. 'But we can handle our security on our own. Mr Marley manages to scare off any would-be burglars. In fact, he enjoys giving them a fright. Payback, he says.'

'Oh well. Bear me in mind if anything changes.'

The monster fairies meanwhile had made friends with Quasimodo. The French boy sat with rapt attention as they tied numerous colourful ribbons in his matted hair, making him resemble a crooked maypole. He was delighted by his reflection when Inky held up a hand mirror for him to inspect their work. 'Pretty!' he declared.

'Where's he going to sleep?' asked Mel.

Cain raked at his ear with a stout forefinger. 'That's a bit of a problem, I grant you. We're running out of space with Mowgli staying here. I think we'd better put him in with you.'

'Me? But I already share with the monster fairies!'

'And they are getting on so well with him. Perfect.'

Mel scowled at his cheese sandwich. Each twin had their own room, as did the girls; it didn't seem fair that four of them had to squeeze in one room.

'Golly, that sounds fun!' exclaimed the irrepressible Wilkins. 'You could have a midnight feast!'

'I suppose you'd like to stay the night too?' asked Mel sourly.

'Oh could I? That would be smashing. Then I could meet Mr Abel and the pack. Can I borrow a toothbrush?'

'I have a spare,' offered Eve. She managed to break so many she had several back-ups.

'Aargh!' Mel groaned. Events were definitely running away from him.

'You all right?' asked Wilkins. 'Not got something stuck in your throat? I've been taught first aid, you know.'

Before Wilkins set out to prove his usefulness by rendering medical assistance, Mel assured him he was fine.

'Mel's just adjusting,' said Cain with a wicked twinkle in his eye. 'He'll be all right in a minute.'

Needing a break from his friends, Mel left the room with the excuse that he was going to organize a mattress and bedding for his unwanted guests. It was not like him to have an attack of the dismals, Mel thought, as he clomped up the stairs. Opening the lavender-scented laundry cupboard, he began sorting through the stack of linen. The twins had invented a steam-powered machine that washed and then wrung out the household sheets. This fearsome object was rigged up in the scullery where it puffed and growled on washdays. Mel was rather scared of it, having almost got his fingers trapped in the rollers, but the fairies enjoyed 'feeding the beast', as they called it and took responsibility for most of the laundry. They were also responsible for the highly perfumed results. Mel sneezed.

'All right, my old cobber?' asked Inky, climbing Mel's leg and hauling himself up to his shoulder.

'Fine.' Mel selected two pillowcases embroidered with silver skulls and handed them to Inky.

'You don't sound fine,' declared Nightie, setting

about a tug-o'-war with a tartan blanket that he was destined to lose.

'It's just that I'm feeling surplus to requirements.'

'You?' Inky began laughing but stopped when he realized that Mel wasn't joking. 'How can you think that?'

'When I first came here, none of you really wanted me. I get it – I really do. I'm not a proper monster like the rest of you. Fine, I was helpful with the battle with the Chief Butler and his armies, but they're gone, my power isn't needed. All I can do is shoot a few sparks at the wolves. I can't bend metal bars like Eve, or shape-shift like Viorica and the twins. I can't drive or cook like the mummy, or carry messages like the raven.'

'But we can't do those things either,' said Nightie, giving up on the blanket and wrestling with a pillow instead. This he managed to drag off its shelf but it ended up on top of him and he had to be rescued.

'Yes, but at least you look like a real monster – you know, short and . . . and unusual looking. You've never had to argue you deserve a place here.'

'Make no bones about it, Mel: we're ugly and proud of it!' declared Inky.

'And that new boy, he's different too. Nobody would think him ordinary. You'll all accept him right off. Sometimes I feel like some of you think I shouldn't really be here.'

'We don't!' squeaked Nightie.

'No, but Viorica and Abel believe that, I can tell. As does anyone who comes to the front door.'

All necessary items located, Mel and the fairies carried or dragged the bedding into the boys' room.

'Do you think I should give up the bed to Quasimodo? He's been in gaol so he might appreciate a soft mattress,' asked Mel as he made up a second bed on the floor.

'You can join us in here if you like,' offered Inky from under the bedstead.

'And if you don't mind getting your hair stuck in the springs,' added Nightie.

'Thanks for the offer but I'll be comfortable enough over here.' Mel plumped the pillow. 'I'll only be sharing with Fred Wilkins for one night, if I'm lucky.'

'I hope Quasi doesn't snore. He looks like he might snore,' said Nightie thoughtfully. 'Nose a bit crooked, like.' He pushed his own to one side to demonstrate.

'He can't help it,' said Inky. 'Got hit in the face by a bell when he was learning the ropes, he told me.'

'He said that much to you in English? That's amazing!' exclaimed Mel.

'Not that amazing. All he said was "bell" then mimed smashing his own conk. He's a good sort, doesn't mind you laughing at him.'

Mel knew that the issue of his welcome in the house wasn't going to be sorted with these two cheerful fairies. They were too happy being who they were to understand why Mel might feel he didn't fit. 'We should go back down. Cain was going to start questioning Quasimodo after tea and I'd like to be there for that. Thanks for talking to me, fairies.'

'Never forget, you're a top chap.' Inky scampered out.

'A monster's best friend,' added Nightie, following on after.

'But not really one of you though,' sighed Mel, closing the bedroom door.

Chapter Six
Hostage

Abel, Mowgli and the wolves had returned by the time Mel came back to the drawing room. He was secretly pleased to discover the pack did not consider Wilkins an alpha either. They were jumping all over the policeman and blasting him with wafts of their hot, smelly breath. Such was the pandemonium around the tea tray that Quasimodo had retreated to the mantelpiece, where he crouched like a large bird of prey roosting on an inadequate twig. He moaned softly as he saw his friend go under a pile of bodies with enthusiastic tails. Sugar cubes shot like blunderbuss pellets in all directions as a paw sent the tea tray flying.

'Fred!' cried Quasimodo. 'They eat Fred!'

Wilkins waved his hand valiantly from under the scrum. 'It's all right, Quasi: they're just playing. They only want to be fri– ow! –ends.'

Leaning against the other end of the chimneypiece, arms crossed, Abel had been rather enjoying the ravaging of the human guest, but seeing that it was seriously upsetting the French boy, he gave a piercing whistle. 'You will back off, sirs!'

Grey Wolf reinforced the command with a howl. Mowgli meanwhile squatted on the hearthrug like a carpet seller in the Great Bazaar of Lahore, watching the antics as if it were passing trade, none of his concern. The monster fairies huddled behind him where they felt safest. Swift Bite, Growler and Little Akela reluctantly moved off their new playmate, leaving a rumpled Wilkins flat on his back, limp like seaweed beached as the tide retreats, uniform in ragged fronds, well beyond saving after this second attack on him in one eventful afternoon. Eve scooped him up and gently placed him on the sofa to recover.

'Are you really all right, Frédérique?' she asked.

'Fine – fine,' gasped Wilkins. 'They've licked me into shape, that I can tell you.' Ruefully he looked at his ripped trousers. 'Though I am going to catch it from my sarge. He's a stickler for a tidy turnout.'

'Now the fun and games are over,' said Cain, helping Quasimodo down from the shelf, 'let's see what this boy can tell us about the thief.'

'*Oui*, we must clear his name and catch the real culprit,' agreed Eve.

Mel shooed the three younger wolves out into the

hallway and shut the door smartly on their whines.

'Mademoiselle Frankenstein, if you would be so kind as to act as interpreter,' requested Abel, picking up the statuettes Quasimodo had displaced in his flight to higher ground.

'Ask him what the thief came to steal,' suggested Mel.

'And what he looks like,' added Wilkins. 'All we've got on the Wanted poster at the moment is "Suspect thought to be an old man; looks like a grey blur; smells rotten".'

'We think he can also travel in time,' explained Eve, wanting to be as helpful as possible to her new friend.

'Mademoiselle, we weren't going to share that with the authorities until we had confirmation,' said Abel, frowning as he shovelled pieces of a china dog into the coal scuttle.

Wilkins sat up. 'By the great Sir Robert! A time traveller!' His cheerful expression turned to one of horror. 'Hang on: that makes him pretty much unstoppable. Oh crumbs, the sarge really won't like that.'

Abel smiled wryly at this understatement. 'I'm afraid the Police Commissioner himself will find the news disturbing.'

'I'd say it makes him the most dangerous cove in the world. He slips in and out before you have a chance to say Newgate Gaol,' added Cain.

'So I suggest we keep it between ourselves for now. No point raising unnecessary alarm.'

Wilkins nodded, quite overawed by Abel's upper-class manner. Used to being in a chain of command, the policeman assumed Abel to be the Chief Constable of the Monster Resistance, as long as he was in that elegant brother form, that was. Mel wondered if Wilkins knew about the whole body-swapping routine the twins had going on. Eve would probably gush out that secret too to impress him, given half a chance.

Despondently, Mel perched on a padded footstool at the edge of the circle around Quasimodo, rubbing at one of his scratches obtained from an earlier bout with the wolves. He listened as Eve questioned Quasimodo about his home in the cathedral, what had happened on the night when the traveller had come, what he remembered. The boy's answers needed little translation as he acted most of them out to accompany his words. He had been sleeping. Someone had trod on his hand. He had grasped an ankle and held on. He had been very cold and confused for a long, long time. The thief had made him carry a smiley lady picture and they had gone place to place – Quasimodo had not known what else to do. Then the thief had left him in the zoo with a crate of fruit. The answer to part of Quasimodo's mystery suddenly became obvious to Mel.

'Ask him when he is from – what year.'

'You think he is a time traveller too?' said Eve.

'We've assumed there's only one, but what if the thief can carry not just things but *people* with him?'

'Then we would get a boy, speaking an old version of French, washed up in Regent's Park. That's brilliant!' exclaimed Abel.

'It is awful,' said Eve. 'He has been taken from all he knows.'

'But from what he said earlier he wasn't having that nice a time in old Paris,' Mel reminded her. 'Go on: ask him. Let's see if I'm right.'

Eve went back to questioning Quasimodo. 'He thinks the year is 1482 though he is not sure. Mel is right: he has been dragged out of his time to the present.'

'Our present, not his,' said Cain. 'With a time machine, every moment can be the here and now. It's very democratic that way.' He exchanged a gleeful look with his brother. 'Oh how we love paradoxes!'

'I'm glad someone is enjoying them because they don't help Quasimodo.' Mel shivered, thinking of all the centuries separating the boy from his own time. Only the mummy might have a chance of understanding how that felt. 'What can we do about it?'

Mowgli unfolded from his resting position on his haunches to stand up. 'It is as clear as the eye of the great Bagheera himself: we hunt down the thief and return the boy to his time.'

'If he wants to go,' added Cain. 'Can't see that he does any harm staying here.'

Quasimodo cocked his head to one side like a robin perched on a spade, aware they were talking about him but not following the conversation.

'What about changing history? I heard that with time travel you could make a frightful mess of things, like killing your own grandfather and stopping yourself being born?' asked Mel. 'Surely it can't be as simple as keeping him if we feel like it?'

'I suppose we could worry about that,' said Cain, 'but my gut tells me that time is more robust than that. If we've changed it, we are already living it, if you get me.'

'So are you saying there is only one outcome – the one we are living? But what about the two versions of what happened to the queen's crown that Eve and I witnessed?'

Cain shrugged. 'You got me there. I'm not sure. We'll have to experiment.'

'But –!'

Abel held up a forefinger. 'We'll do no such thing.'

Phew! Mel was surprised but pleased to find Cain's twin was reining him in – but only briefly, because Abel continued:

'We have no need to experiment as someone is doing that for us in many places at multiple times, though it does appear he is concentrating on our "now". It makes me wonder if the time machine must always return to the era of its own making to reset the clock? There would be some logic to that and it would explain why he keeps cropping up here. We must make a careful study of the changes that result from his actions.'

'And I have another question.' Cain spun the ornamental globe that sat on a side table; it miraculously had missed being overset by the wolves' romp. His finger traced the known paths the thief had taken – Russia, France, England. 'Granted this cove can travel in time, but how does he get around from place to place so darned quickly?'

'I would posit, brother, that in the future travel is very much faster,' mused Abel. 'Think how far we have come since the beginning of the century when the fastest conveyance was the mail coach, top speed an average of ten miles an hour. It used to take days to reach Scotland. Now you can travel from London to Edinburgh on a steam train in eight and a half hours.'

Once the brothers started this kind of speculation they would be absorbed by it for days.

'I know you like theories,' said Mel, 'but can't you see that while you are working out the science behind it all, we're only getting further and further away from catching him? He can move much faster than us – and at different times. We don't stand a chance.'

'Not true, Mel,' replied Cain. 'You see there's something we already know. Like any thief he likes nicking stuff and looks for his chance. He's not really quicker than us – it just seems that way. That's what's going to do for him.'

'How do you mean?'

'Take the queen's diamond.'

'He already has.'

Cain smiled. 'Yes, but I think what he really did is nab it off her head, go back – or forward – to a quiet moment in the same spot to make the swap with the orange and then pop back to pretty much the same moment he left. For him it all passes quite slowly. It's only us that see it as a super-human blur.'

Mel scratched his head. 'So?'

'What Cain sahib means,' said Mowgli, 'is that like any prey he can be trapped when you know his hunting patterns. We stake out something he wants and make sure we stop him leaving.'

'So what does he want next?' asked Eve.

'We can see he likes the finest things and he's already got the Second Star of India. I can't see him stopping until he's got the First, can you?' said Cain.

'We just need to create the perfect stealing opportunity to lure him in – make it known that we are moving the sceptre to keep it safe,' said Abel.

'He pops up in our moment and, hey presto, we tackle him.'

'We get the thief and the time machine in one fell swoop.'

'The police get their man.' Cain nodded to Wilkins.

'And we get a fascinating chance to study how he did it.' Abel and Cain looked very pleased with themselves.

'I can see that it sounds like a good plan,' said Mel, 'but somehow I don't think we've got time on our side.'

The time traveller shuffled from his scullery past the two muscled men occupying the best seats in his kitchen to put another rasher of bacon in the frying pan.

'I like mine well done,' said one of the Inventor's enforcers. 'Crispy – like your cat will be if you don't do what we say.' His companion laughed, sounding like a squeaky bicycle freewheeling down Hampstead Hill. Both men were dressed in clothes familiar around the dockyard: coarse clothing, heavy boots, flat caps. The only sign that they were flourishing in the Inventor's service were the thick gold rings they both wore, eight a-piece, though Krook suspected they acted as much as weapons as indications of wealth.

Tail lashing in silent outrage, Lady Jane stared at the invaders from the top of the cupboard where she had retreated when the men had moved in with their bulldog. This charmer, rejoicing under the picturesque name of Dog, was lying under the kitchen table, alert for any scraps that might drop, or could be snatched from unwary fingers. Nursing a bandage on his left hand, Krook knew now to take more care.

'I'll have to go out and get some more meat,' he said plaintively, seeing the last of his plunder going into the pan. He hadn't yet had his own breakfast and wasn't used to going without.

'Stay where you are!' warned the bacon eater. 'We're to keep you here until you get your orders.'

As if the words conjured that very thing, there came the slap of an envelope hitting the doormat and the snap closed of the letterbox. Krook took a step to go to fetch it but was hauled back by his guard.

'I'll get it. Bacon, chop-chop!'

Returning to the pan, Krook waited with a bitter show of humility while the enforcer fetched the letter, opened it and read the contents. 'This is what we've been waiting for. We know where the target is going to be. The old man is to kidnap Melchizedek Foster tonight and take him back in time. We're to leave a ransom note at the scene. Then the old man's to return here ten minutes later to confirm the job's done – cat safe – everyone happy.'

Own mouth watering, Krook served the last nicely blackened rashers to the men. 'What kind of monster am I kidnapping?'

'Here you go.' The thug tossed the letter to him. Krook quickly read the description. Melchizedek Foster. Was he unusually strong or incredibly tall? No to both. Did he change shape? Negative. As far as Krook could work out, Melchizedek Foster could produce a few electrostatic sparks, but then so could Lady Jane when you stroked her fur. The only odd thing about the boy was that he resided with so many monsters. Was he some kind of pet? Or lunch?

Krook did not consider himself a bad man. Greedy, yes, but he had no appetite for inflicting bodily harm on anyone. He would clearly be doing the boy a favour by liberating him from this house of monsters, at the same time as fulfilling the Inventor's order. Best of all, he would be doing it at very little risk to himself as even an old man could surely subdue one small boy?

Mel had the uncanny feeling that he was being watched. He couldn't put his finger on it, had no evidence that his hunch had any foundation, yet he distinctly felt a tickling sensation on the back of his neck. He'd learned to trust the itch when he'd lived at Wackford Squeers's Orphanage. If ever he had sneaked off to a quiet corner of the building Mel had trusted that feeling to warn him of Squeers's imminent arrival with his birch cane. Nine times out of ten, Mel had escaped a beating by having an approved moralizing text open on his knee, hiding the Boy's Own adventure magazine he had scavenged from Squeers's rubbish bin. The tenth time, Squeers would whack him anyway just because he could.

'Eve, do you have the feeling we are being followed?' asked Mel as they headed home from their shift on duty at the Tower of London. On the request of the Monster Resistance, the queen had ordered that the sceptre be moved from the vault holding the Crown Jewels to a strong room so it could await transport to the Bank of England – at least that was the story given out to the press. A fake sceptre had been substituted for the real thing just in case something went wrong. The trap was baited and now all they had to do was mount a twenty-four-hour watch to catch the time thief when he popped in to this less secure location to take it.

'No, I don't feel that, but then, people always look at me and trail me down the street to get a closer look. I think they must find me very attractive. It can be embarrassing.' Blushing, Eve scattered a few crumbs she had saved for the ravens hopping about the Tower lawn. Their raven was undercover among them but Mel could pick him out easily as he was the only one in the habit of croaking 'Nevermore' when presented with a particularly juicy tidbit.

Mel was pleased for Eve that she thought that was the reason she garnered so much attention. 'Well, they don't normally look at me at all but still I think that maybe someone is – and not just today – yesterday as well.'

Sensitive to the genuine concern in his voice, Eve stood for a moment surveying the crowds visiting the ancient building. The White Tower rose like a sheer chalk cliff from a grass ocean. Black-hatted, red-jacketed beefeaters marched around the perimeter, busy little coastguard vessels patrolling the inland waters. Families and overseas visitors were ferried to and fro from Tower Green to royal dungeons.

'I can't see anyone looking at you. Do you still feel it?' Eve asked.

Mel shook his head. 'No. At least, not as strongly. Maybe I'm just imagining it? You probably think I'm silly. I mean, who's the least bit interested in me?'

'You're not silly. You should always listen to your instincts, Mel: that's what my father taught me.'

'My instincts aren't very helpful. They just give me a tingly feeling down my spine without explaining why.'

'I get a tingly feeling too very often.' Eve started walking again towards the Underground station. 'Especially when Frédérique smiles at me.'

'I don't think that's quite the same thing, Eve.' Mel was getting somewhat tired of hearing how wonderful the constable was.

'Do you think he will come to supper again tonight?'

'He's come every day since he slept that night in my room so I think the chance is quite high, don't you?'

'Oh good.' Eve smiled into the middle distance, thoughts dancing in some romantic scene which Mel bet involved flowers, soft music and candlelight. 'Do you think he likes me?'

Now this was trickier. Mel had been watching Fred Wilkins closely and, as far as he could make out, the policemen was equally enamoured of all the inhabitants of the Jekylls' house. He was in love with the idea of being a monster rather than a particular one. 'Of course he likes you. I think he likes all of us.'

'I'm so glad. Isn't he just adorable? And brave?'

'Yes, he's adorable and brave.' Mel had learned his role in these conversations was just to echo Eve's opinion. She wasn't really listening to him.

'He has a lovely voice.'

'But snores like a rhino.' It had turned out that Quasimodo made a most unobjectionable roommate whereas the constable kept them all awake. He had also spread out on his back like a starfish, causing Mel to spend that particular night on the bare floorboards rather than the mattress.

'What was that?'

'I said he's as tuneful as a piano.'

Eve nodded happily. 'I do love it when he whistles. He knows all the latest songs, he told me.'

It was perhaps time to make her a little more cautious? 'You do know, don't you, Eve, that he might not be looking for a particular friend among us? He might just want to be friends with all of us?'

'I know – and isn't that lovely of him: to want to like all of us even though Viorica did try to bite him the other evening. He was most understanding.'

That confrontation had resulted in Eve leaping to her swain's defence and shattering the lower pane as she threw the vampire out of the dining-room window. Viorica was still sulking in bat form in the stables over that slight to her dignity.

104

'You will be able to keep your mind on the job tomorrow, won't you?' asked Mel. 'You're the one who has to keep hold of the thief when we catch him.'

'Do you think Frédérique will be there to see me do it?'

'Yes.'

'What shall I wear?' Eve caught sight of herself in the window of a hat shop. 'Do you think I need a new bonnet?'

Good grief. 'I think you should wear your uniform as usual.' Her face fell. 'Really. You look lovely in it.'

'I do?' Eve turned her gaze back to a pink hat covered in roses. 'But maybe it needs brightening up?'

Mel took a few paces away from her. He loved Eve but frankly this was beginning to annoy him. If he heard one more word about how wonderful the constable was, he would scream.

But then he screamed anyway.

Chapter Seven

Fallen Among Thieves

Cold. That was Mel's strongest impression. His lips were numb, eyes frozen in their sockets, fingers stiff. Everything around him was moving so fast he could see nothing but a swirl of colours. He had once witnessed a tornado at sea, but this was like sailing right into the heart of it, the wall of water rising on all sides. Wrenching his neck down against a gale force wind, he found a still spot in the confusion: the twiggy end of a broom. Sitting astride the handle was an old man dressed in a coarse tweed suit, long grey hair flapping behind him. His left hand was clutching Mel's collar. To one end of the broom was strapped an intricate device of golden cogs and pulleys set inside what looked like a carriage clock housing. The hands on the dial were spinning backwards, a counter clicking through the days, months and years.

Mel opened his mouth to speak but his words were left in tomorrow before he could form a sentence. The time thief had him. What could he do? He had to make the man stop before Mel lost contact with everything he knew. Perhaps if he made the man drop him? Remembering how he had forced the wolves to let go, Mel reached for his supercharged power, put his hand over the fingers gripping his throat and released a bolt. Light flared.

'Aaargh!' shrieked the man.

The walls of the time tornado shot upwards like a sudden rise of the curtain at the theatre. The world screeched to a halt, objects blurred – rocking for a split second – before firming. A little warmth seeped back into the air. Mel landed in a heap.

'You fool! You fool! Look what you did! You broke it!' The thief was shaking his wrist, still feeling the after-effects of Mel's electric shock. 'I was aiming for 1815 but you've dumped us in . . .' he checked the dial, '1835! I'm alive in 1835. I don't want to be here again! I don't like it!'

Mel gaped at the man who had kidnapped him. They were still in the middle of Tower Hill, but now in falling snow. Fortunately, they had stopped in the night-time so there were few people around to notice two people drop out of the future, one riding a time broom. Mel blinked flakes off his eyelashes. 'Please, sir, if you don't like it now, take us back to 1895.' He didn't know if the man would hurt him or not, but talking him round seemed the best strategy.

'Don't you understand? I can't! That thing you did – I felt it run down my arm and finger into the machine. That was the flash.' The man thrust the broom handle towards Mel. 'Go on: mend it – mend it at once!'

'All right, all right: I'll try!' The man looked as though he was going to throttle Mel if he didn't attempt this. There was enough moonlight to see the little hook catch on the door to the time machine. Trying to shelter it from the snow, Mel opened the casing and peered inside. Despite being packed full of electric life force, Mel knew very little about his own strength. The Jekylls were really the experts on electricity, and they had warned him it was dangerous stuff. How Mel was able to hold so much without coming to harm, the twins hadn't yet discovered.

He stroked the mechanism with a cautious index finger. The cogs looked in working order, though there appeared to be a smattering of grit that sparkled on his fingertip. Powdered glass? 'Are you sure I did something?'

'Can't you smell that?' The old man stamped his foot, leaving a pit in the snowdrift by the shop doorway. 'You did it – you did, you did, you did!'

There was a slight taint of burning in the casing, that was true. Mel tried sending more power into the machine but it just produced a shower of sparks and more burning.

'Stop it!' screeched the thief, putting out the fire with a handful of snow. 'You're making it worse!'

'Now hang on a moment, Mr Time Thief: you are the one who did something first. You grabbed me and dragged me here. You can hardly expect me not to try to stop you kidnapping me!'

'But can't you see: neither of us can ever get home now you've broken it!'

'Oh, so it's my fault is it?'

'Yes, it jolly well is! I've got someone waiting for her dinner at home. I can't stay here! I've got to get it mended. But who knows anything about machines in this day and age?'

'Look, we appear to be in the fix together,' said Mel, kicking aside his panic and trying for reasonable. Survival came first and it was never safe in any era to stop for long in this part of the city. 'It's snowing. We're attracting attention from those men over there so why don't we get off the street and go somewhere to work this out?'

But the time thief was lost in his own mutterings. 'Fara-diddle, Fara-by – it was something like that? Oh why didn't I pay attention when I read the newspapers?'

The three ruffians Mel had spotted decided to move from the doorway of the tavern where they had been lurking and head towards the rather more interesting golden gleam on the end of the broomstick. Mel plucked the old man's sleeve. 'Sir, we've got to move!'

The thief looked up and saw the men approaching. 'They mustn't get the time machine!' He shoved Mel towards the three. 'Here, have this boy!' With a speed surprising for his age, he unstrapped the time machine from the broom, shoved the handle in Mel's hands, and scuttled off into an alleyway.

'Hey, wait!' But it was too late: the men were upon him. Mel took firm hold on the broom. 'Don't come any closer!' He swished the twiggy end in their direction. This really wasn't going to end well.

'Listen to him!' scoffed one rotter, dressed finer than the others in white military trousers and ragged jacket. 'He thinks a chalk-faced kid with a broom is going to scare off Bill Sikes!'

The biggest of the three smiled evilly. 'It'll take a lot more than that to scare me, Toby Crackit. Out of the way, boy, go sweep a crossing and let me catch that vicious old skeleton – the one who ran off and left you in the lurch.'

'I can't let you do that.' Mel stood on guard at the entrance to the alley, broom held crossways. He tried sending a spark down the shaft but wood didn't conduct electricity.

'Bill, the old 'un is getting away with that gold clock,' said the third, pulling a club from a capacious pocket in his overcoat. He took a swipe at Mel who moved quickly to intercept the club with the broom, arms buckling under the blow, knees bending. Slipping a little on the ice below the new-fallen snow, Mel felt himself giving under the pressure. Taking advantage of Mel's position, Bill kicked one end of the broom out of Mel's hand.

'You should've got out of the way while you had a chance, boy.' A fist struck Mel in the side of the head. Pain flashed temple to temple. Mel span and collided with the alley wall. Losing consciousness, he felt quick fingers rifle his pockets, taking everything. Blackness descended as feet ran off down the alley.

'Hullo, my covey! Thinking of offering yourself as a doorstop?'

Mel opened his eyes. A blurred face hovered over him: a pale oval surrounded by brown hair, protruding ears, hat perched to one side.

''Cause if you were, you could find a better place to lie than this. You'll be run over by the drayman's cart in half a tick.'

A hand appeared before Mel's nose. Reaching up to take it, Mel let himself be pulled to his feet. A horse lumbered past a second later, pulling a wagon stacked with barrels.

'My eyes, you are in a bad way!' The helpful boy brushed him down, dislodging the snow from his clothes. 'You've got a lump on your forehead.'

Mel discovered that was the case.

'And you don't look too well, if you don't mind me observing.'

'I don't feel well.'

'Set on by footpads, eh? Not a nice part of town, this.' The boy shook back his sleeves. He was wearing a man's jacket, the tails of which trailed on the ground and the cuffs overshot his hands by several inches. 'You probably need a place to stay?'

Mel supposed he did.

'I know just the thing. I'm friends with a 'spectable old gentleman who lives near here. He gives boys lodgings when they fall on hard times.'

'I definitely have fallen on a hard time.'

'Then you must come with me.'

Mel's wits were slowly returning like doves circling back to the cot. 'But won't he mind? I mean, the thieves have stolen all my money.' He blew on his numb fingertips.

The boy waved that away with a waft of his sleeve. 'Don't fret your eyelids on that score. He's always happy to meet a new pal. You'll see.'

Mel was no green boy in London. He wasn't so sure that the offer would turn out to be free in the long run but for the moment he had to hope he would be welcome. The boy seemed genuine enough and Mel needed somewhere to recover from the blow to his head and make a new plan. Maybe he'd get a brief reprieve from the winter streets? 'I'd like to meet him then. I'm Mel Foster.'

Seeing Mel was still weaving on his feet, the boy took his elbow. 'Pleased to meet you, Mel Foster. I'm Jack Dawkins, though my friends call me Dodger, the Artful Dodger.'

The Dodger led Mel sure-footed through the back alleys to Spitalfields. Mel knew these streets from 1895. Though the plan was the same, his were a lot cleaner thanks to the introduction mid-century of the network of sewers. People in this time wore funny clothes too, especially the men. Gone were the sober three-piece suits of Mel's day; in their place were long-tailed jackets, trousers in many colours and extravagant cravats, making the wearers look like a lot of white-breasted birds hoping about the pavements. As for the women, he'd never seen such ridiculous bonnets obscuring their vision like blinkers on racehorses.

But none of this was going to get him back to his own era. Where had the thief gone? And how was Mel to find him when he didn't even know his name?

Faradiddle – the time thief had mentioned going to see someone called Faradiddle. Or was that the blow to the head still talking?

'Dodger, do you know a man called Faradiddle?'

Dodger stopped by a bookstall and eyed a gentleman sheltering under the awning, lost in contemplation of a leather-bound tome he had selected from a box of books. 'Oh yes, me and him are best pals. Dine together every Tuesday at the Houses of Parliament, we do.'

'So that's a "no" then.'

Dodger chuckled good-humouredly and turned shrewd dark eyes on Mel. 'So you're not from the country? I thought you was, or maybe just off a ship with them strange togs.'

Mel looked down and realized he was still wearing his Monster Resistance uniform of fitted black jacket and trousers. 'No, I'm from around here.'

'Ain't seen you before.'

'I've been busy.'

'You been in service then to some odd gent who likes his servant dressed like the grim reaper, eh? Don't blame you for running off.'

Mel shrugged, deciding this guess was as good as any. The clothes did look a little like the livery of a house in mourning.

Dodger tucked his thumbs in his jacket's breast pockets, which hung near his waist. 'But the old man I mentioned is a good mate of mine and, times being what they are, sometimes he has to sail a bit on the windy side of the law.'

'So many of us do,' agreed Mel, thinking of the activities he had got up to with Cain Jekyll, a little housebreaking and a side serving of sleight of hand in case of emergencies.

'Are you able to keep your mouth shut, that's what I

need to know? To protect my friend.'

'Trust me: I can keep a secret.'

'All right then.' With a flash of a grin, Dodger darted down an evil-smelling lane and rapped on the door of a lodgings house. The alley was so narrow, no snow had found its way down here. Not waiting for an answer, he ushered Mel inside. 'Go right to the top.'

Taking care on the rotten staircase, which missed half of its treads, Mel climbed to the top floor. His head was pounding like a whole party of Grimm's dwarves had moved in and started mining operations. He was looking forward to lying down.

'Is that you, Dodger?' called a man's high-pitched voice.

'Yes, Fagin. And I've brought a new pal.'

The door opened and a tall stick of a man stood in the entrance, unkempt red hair straggling around his face, ragged dressing gown dragging on the dirty floor. 'Oh, my dear, I always like to make the acquaintance of your pals. And who do we have the very great pleasure of meeting?' He gave Mel a bow as he pulled him inside and banged the door closed.

'This here is Master Mel Foster.' Dodger strutted round the room, dropping a few snuffboxes from his pockets on to the wonky table. 'But, Fagin, he ain't green. He's London, not country bred.'

Fagin's gaze sharpened, eyes sparkling with pleasure. 'Oh well, we can work with that too, can't we, my dear?

Now, Master Foster, take a seat. Consider yourself at home. We were about to have breakfast.'

Mel would have preferred to go straight to being horizontal but he vaguely remembered that you should attempt to stay awake if you had a head wound. Besides he wanted to find out more about these people who had so instantly opened their home to him. 'Thank you, sir.'

Fagin put a large frying pan on the cracked stovetop. 'Where are you from exactly, if that is not too bold a question to ask so early on in our acquaintance?'

Mel thought fast. 'An orphanage not far from here.' Or it would be in sixty years' time.

'So no family. No friends?' Fagin juggled four eggs from a wire basket on the mantelpiece.

'Oh, no family – some friends, but they're not here at the moment.'

Fagin lifted an enquiring brow to Dodger.

'He was flat on his back, Fagin. Some vicious footpads had turned him over.' For some reason, Dodger nodded at the wall, but Fagin seemed to understand. 'I couldn't leave him there, could I? He'd've frozen to death before morning, poor kid.'

Fagin muttered something as he broke the eggs into the pan, whisking them with a fork.

'He could make a fine fogel-hunter with the right training.'

So that was the windy side of the law the Dodger mentioned. Mel wasn't that surprised that they stole handkerchiefs, or fogels, for a living. In difficult times, it wasn't that great a sin, after all, not if the alternative was starving. Mel rubbed his temples. Maybe he had been exceptionally lucky the Dodger had found him? Perhaps this little gang of thieves were the very people to help him steal back the time machine?

'You're very clever this morning, Dodger.' Fagin slapped a plate of scrambled eggs in front of the boys. 'Get that down you, Dodger, then it's time to pad the hoof. Master Foster can rest here for the day. We'll discuss how to help him when he's had a chance to recover. I've got an appointment in the city with a particular friend of mine. Nancy can keep an eye on him.' He thumped the chimneypiece.

A girl with curly brown hair and a pale, sleepy face put her head through a hole in the brickwork from the next room. 'What you want, you old villain?'

'Ah, Nancy my dear, how charming you are this morning.'

She snorted and yawned. 'Been up all night, ain't I? Anyway, what you want? Bill's only just got back in and we both need some shut-eye.'

'The boy here: you'll look after him for me, won't you? Make sure he has everything he needs? He took a knock last night, didn't he, my dear. Isn't quite feeling top of the trees today.'

Nancy's eyes swept Mel, assessing. 'Hullo there. You feeling poorly?'

Mel rose from his stool and bowed. 'I've had better days, miss.'

Nancy preened a little, fluffing her hair. 'Nice manners this one, Fagin. Yes I'll watch him. Looks to me though like nothing a good sleep won't fix. Little 'un, you sing out if you need old Nance, all right?'

Mel estimated she was barely ten years older than him so 'old' seemed a little overstating the case. 'Yes, miss.'

'You get some shut-eye then I'll come and make you a nice cup of tea.'

Mel returned her smile. She really did seem a friendly kind of girl. 'Oh, I don't want to be any trouble.'

'It's no trouble at all. Toodle-oo then.' She retreated, dropping the curtain over the gap between the rooms. Mel heard the rumble of an unseen man next door, Nancy replying, then they fell silent.

'I'm off,' said Dodger, wiping the plate clean with a crust of bread. 'I'm meeting Charley in Bethnal Green.'

'Any word on Jim?' asked Fagin, warming his gin-and-water by inserting into the cup a poker that had been lying on the coals. The liquid hissed and spat like Viorica when she was angry.

'The traps have got him so it's all over with him.' Dodger tipped his hat upright, though it immediately slipped again only to be stopped from tumbling off by the lucky proportion of his ears.

Could that mean one of their number was facing the noose?

Fagin shook out a sack for Mel to lie on and gestured for him to curl up. He threw another sack over Mel by way of a blanket. 'I'll ask Betsy to take him a basket – a pie and a jug of something special. He'll go to the nipping jig with a feast to warm his last hours.'

'You're a generous old gentleman, Fagin,' said Dodger. 'Send him my best.'

The door banged behind the thieves. Eyes closing, Mel's thoughts turned to poor Jim. Nipping jig was a term for hanging. Fagin could only send him a basket, not bail him from gaol, a timely reminder of the severe penalties facing anyone caught stealing in 1835. But Mel needed their help if he was going to get back home. He couldn't trace Krook without some local knowledge, nor break in to get the time machine on his own. Fagin was a slippery customer but Nancy and Dodger seemed friendly enough. Maybe once they got to know him better, they'd be willing to run the risk with him? But would it be fair to ask them?

Jacob Marley blanched an even paler white as the front door flew back on its hinges before he could open it. 'My dear madam!'

Eve stormed right through him, a punnet of raspberries in hand. 'Cain! Abel! The time thief has Mel Foster!'

'Oh woe! Doom is upon us!' wailed Marley, turning in ever decreasing circles so that his chain quite covered him, like thread does a bobbin on a spinning wheel.

Cain charged in from the courtyard bringing a trail of panting wolves at his heels. Mowgli slid down the banister. Abel emerged from the library, book in hand. The mummy entered at a run from the kitchen, brandishing a wooden spoon, which showered chocolate sauce on to an oblivious Inky and Nightie clinging to his legs. Quasimodo swung from the rope they had rigged for him from the top floor rail to the foyer. Only Viorica and the Raven were missing, on duty at the Tower.

'What's happened?' asked Cain.

'The thief – he wasn't after the sceptre: he was after Mel Foster.' Eve thrust the punnet at Cain, spilling raspberries over the tiles.

'Look: there's a note. He's never left a note before.' Cain passed it to Abel, who unfolded it, checking for clues in the penmanship and quality of the paper.

'*To Her Majesty Queen Victoria and her ministers,*' he read. '*We have taken Melchizedek Foster and sent him far back in time, never to return. That proves that no one is safe from us: we can reach anyone, no matter how secure they believe themselves to be, and put them in the past or the future as we see fit. The Empire is now at our mercy. Much worse will follow if you do not do exactly as we say. As a first step, we demand a*

120

ransom for the future safety of all those you hold dear,
one million pounds, delivered to the following bank in
Switzerland by midnight on Friday.'

Quasimodo moaned and hugged himself, picking up on the distress in the hall even if not sure of the cause.

'Her Majesty isn't going to like that,' said Cain. 'This is blackmail. She won't cough up.'

'But he's made his point though, hasn't he?' said Abel. The point is that none of us are safe. If it was Mel today, it might be the Prince of Wales tomorrow.'

'But why start with Mel and not the prince, then?'

'It reeks to me of the settling of old scores. Mel Foster is the Inventor's son and number one enemy since Mel defeated the Demon Butler. I'd wager that the Inventor must be the one behind this plot as he was the one before.'

'But what can we do to save Mel Foster? I will not accept that he is never to return,' said Eve. Yes, she was worried for everyone's future, but mainly she was concerned about the present crisis, not the next one.

Mowgli took the punnet and held it out to Grey Wolf. The wolf examined both the basket and the raspberries then yipped his verdict.

'The same man as was present at the other thefts filled this basket, sahibs,' said Mowgli, 'but the note has been touched by another. The smell is expensive – cologne, laundered shirt, something briny. The writer has recently come from the sea.'

121

Abel tapped his fingers on his crossed forearms. 'The pattern changes.'

'He's palled up with someone?' said Cain.

Eve knew she should care about these deductions but she was burning to do something for her friend. She wanted to punch a fist through a wall and drag Mel back to safety.

'Mel Foster gone?' asked Quasimodo, his slower grasp of English now catching up with the others.

'*Oui*. He has been taken – like you were.'

Quasimodo visibly shook in his shoes. 'My fault. Bad old man. Very bad. He live near river. Smell bad there too.'

The monsters in the foyer fell silent. 'You know where he lives?' asked Abel, trying not to spook Quasimodo. The twin looked like he would prefer to shake Quasimodo and shout 'WHY DIDN'T YOU SAY SO!'

'He not think I see these things. We stop – go – stop – on broom. I think he is a witch.'

'More like a "which", as in "which century?"' muttered Cain for his brother's benefit as no one else was in the mood for puns.

'We get on long metal carriage.' Quasimodo sketched an arc in the air. 'Shoot from Paris to this place. That is witchcraft.'

'So he does use vehicles in the future to get around so quickly. I wonder what they are like?' mused Abel.

'But how do you know where the bad man lives?' asked Eve, returning Quasimodo to the main point before the twins got sidetracked.

'He stop and leave pretty picture.' Quasimodo grimaced in his approximation of the Mona Lisa's smile.

'And where were you?' said Abel.

'In dark cupboard. Smell of boots. He give fish to his cat. Nice cat. I say "leave Quasimodo too" but he scare me. Take me to bear cage and leave me.'

Despite Quasimodo's limited vocabulary, Eve could see the events quite plainly now. The poor boy had been dragged through time from Paris to London, threatened and dumped by the thief. Was that what the villain was doing to Mel right now?

'Why didn't you tell us this before?' asked Abel.

'I scared. Not speak your language.'

'Do you think you can find his house again?' said Cain.

Quasimodo looked to Eve, clearly worried he was going to fail his new friends.

'Just do your best,' she told him.

'The wolves can help, sahib,' said Mowgli. 'If Quasimodo can get us near, we can do the rest.'

Quasimodo nodded. 'I try. It is in London near big river.'

'Good enough.' Cain patted his shoulder.

'And if we get our hands on the thief, what then?' asked Eve.

123

'Leave that to us, mademoiselle, we have our ways,' said Abel.

Eve let that be a comfort to her. She trusted Cain and Abel and knew enough of their characters never to want to find herself on the wrong side of them.

'Meanwhile, we should still keep watch on the sceptre. Remember that time makes no sense in this mystery. Our thief can be in two places at once. We are fighting on multiple fronts. I'll go to the palace with the ransom note.'

Cain put on his flat cap and muffler. 'And I'll go and tell the team at the Tower to keep a look out. We can't lose anyone else to this kidnapper. Fight him off if he grabs you.'

'That didn't do Mel Foster any good,' said Eve. 'He screamed. He struggled.'

'Then we'll just have to get the thief before he gets us, won't we?'

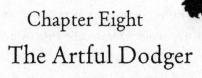

Chapter Eight
The Artful Dodger

Mel wasn't sure what his first day in 1835 would bring him but he suspected nothing good.

Waking to an empty room after several hours of sleep he considered his position. He had lost his only way home. The one glimmer of hope was that the time thief was stranded too. Mel knew what the old man would be doing – finding someone to mend the machine – and that had to narrow down his options. Dodger and his gang might be able to help Mel get hold of the machine once he located it but what he needed now was someone from this decade who knew the experts on time travel. An educated gentleman or lady who took the scientific journals would be just the ticket. His guardian in 1895 was a man of that character: Dr Foster, learned in the medical arts but friendly with many other scientists. Mel did a quick calculation. In this era, the doctor was alive but a little boy, probably chanting his multiplication tables at infant school. Mel needed an adult.

'Who do I know who is grown up in this decade?' Mel wondered aloud. He would have to be ridiculously old to still be alive in 1895.

Or dead. That was it! Jacob Marley wasn't a ghost in 1835 but a living breathing man. Mel and the butler had always got on reasonably well. If Mel explained his position to Mr Marley, surely, after a few warnings of doom and disaster, he would help? All Mel need do was find him.

Before Mel could act on his thought, Nancy entered wearing a rose gown a little stained at the hem. Long curly brown hair tumbled from beneath her frilly cap. 'My, you look better, young man! I can see that sleep did you the power of good.'

Mel rubbed his forehead, finding that the lump had diminished from goose to hen egg size. 'I am much better, thank you.'

'So polite!' Nancy threw open the doors to a cupboard set beside the chimneybreast. 'Now what's that vicious old man keeping for dinner, eh?' There didn't seem to be very much on the shelves but she did manage to find the end of a stale loaf and a garlic sausage, the smell of which reached Mel on the other side of the room as she put it on the table. Mouth watering, he shook off the sack and tidied his clothing. It felt a long while since breakfast.

Nancy banged the cupboard closed. 'You best come and get it before Dodger and Fagin get back. Oops, too late.' With a carefree smile at him, Nancy put three plates on the table, none of them matching.

The Dodger sauntered into the room with his hands stuck in his pockets. 'Afternoon, all. Left any for a poor hard-working gentleman of the roads?' Nancy put the last slice on a plate for him. 'Thanks, Nancy, you're a darling.'

'How's Master Foster?' Dodger took a bite of his supper, chewing with mouth open, speaking through the crumbs. 'You recovered your wits, Doorstop?'

'Half of them at least,' said Mel.

Dodger grinned. 'So, are you going to tell us what brought you to lying flat on your back on Tower Hill?'

Mel wondered how to explain. 'I was brought there by an old man. He . . . um . . . had come to get his clock mended. We were attacked by thieves and he ran off. I really, really need to find him again. It's a matter of life and death.'

The Dodger wiped his sleeve across his mouth, his quick supper over. 'So how you going to find that old cove?'

'I think I know where he may be going with his

clock. I was going to ask someone I believe would help me. A man called Jacob Marley. Do you know him?'

Dodger started to choke. 'Oh my wig, my wig! You want to go for help from Mr Jacob Marley? Jacob Marley of Scrooge and Marley?'

'I suppose that's the same man,' said Mel but he wasn't very sure at all.

'Describe him.'

'Well, he is about Fagin's height but much thinner. Wears his hair in an old-fashioned style, caught back at the nape in a ribbon.' He tried to guess at the colours of the ghost's clothes, which after death had all become shades of white and grey. 'I think he wears a long dark jacket to about here.' He tapped his thigh. 'And a lighter waistcoat with brass buttons. Oh yes, and his nose is large – a little like Wellington's.'

'God bless old beaky,' sighed Nancy. 'He's a man who treats all women like duchesses, they say. What you think, Dodger, is that the old man down on Cheapside?'

'I think it sounds just like him.' Dodger winked at Nancy. 'So, Master Foster, you think that this Jacob Marley will give you a warm welcome, do you? Shall we go and see?'

'If you would just tell me where to find him, I'm sure I can find my own way.' Grateful though he was for a guide, Mel was not keen to make his appeal to Mr Marley with a thief in tow.

'No, no, I wouldn't miss this for the world.'

'Dodger!' Nancy seemed to be reproving him about something but Mel wasn't sure what the undercurrent was between those two.

'I insist. Shake a leg, Master Foster. We've got a kind old gentleman to call on.' Dodger tapped his hat into place and headed for the door.

Mel wasn't much encouraged by the outside of Mr Marley's place of work. In a dingy courtyard off Cheapside, the warehouse had a bold sign over the door in black curly letters, *Scrooge and Marley*, so he knew he was in the right place. The building itself was the opposite of welcoming, as the paintwork was peeling, the windows dirty with very few lights inside even though there were clerks still at their desks.

'I'm not sure this is such a good idea,' said Mel, pulling back.

Dodger was not so faint-hearted. 'Nothing ventured, nothing gained, my covey.' He tugged Mel's sleeve but as they were about evenly matched in height he couldn't dislodge Mel from the lamp post he had grabbed to anchor himself. Snow began falling in new drifts. Lights sprang up in the windows of the grocers and bakers on Cheapside, their goods displayed in piles of oranges, candied fruit, buns and cakes. Holly and ivy wound in festive garlands on many doors. The normally dour people of London smiled in passing, wishing each other season's greetings. Only this little courtyard seemed to have been bypassed by the Christmas spirit. Dodger puffed out his cheeks and tried a different tack. 'Come on, it's Christmas Eve –'

'It is?' Mel hadn't known the actual day though he had guessed they were near the holiday.

The Dodger gave him a funny look. 'Course it is. You still feeling odd from that knock to the canister?'

'No, no, I just forgot.'

'Right. Christmas Eve. Season of goodwill to all men. How about we go up to the door in the guise of carol singers? We give them a burst of a heart-warming song and then, when they are fully in the Christmas mood, Bob's your uncle, we can ask them for help with your problem. How does that sound?'

Mel had to admit it sounded a reasonable plan. He could gauge what sort of man Jacob Marley was at this end of the century from how he greeted a couple of innocent carol singers. Everyone loved a good Christmas song, didn't they? 'Which one shall we sing?'

Dodger scratched his head. 'Not sure I know many, now I come to think of it. Not much of a pew polisher, if you follow me.'

Attendance at Sunday service had been obligatory in Mel's orphanage so his trouser seat had polished a few pews in his time. 'I know some. What about "God rest ye merry gentlemen"?'

The Dodger took off his hat in preparation for receiving a donation for their song and adjusted his overlong jacket. 'I like the sound of that one. You start, I'll join in.'

Mel ascended the three steps leading to the doorway over which the sign was suspended and rapped firmly with the lion-shaped knocker. Hearing footsteps approaching, Mel began to sing:

'God rest ye, merry gentlemen,
Let nothing you dismay!'

Dodger joined in a few beats behind time. 'God bless you merry gentleman, Let's put on a good display!'

The door opened a crack and a kind but anxious face appeared in the gap. It didn't look much like Mr Marley, too young for how Mel had pictured him, but he carried on regardless.

'Remember Christ our Saviour,
Was born on Christmas Day!'

Dodger tagged along behind: 'Remember what's to savour, Plum puddings on Christmas Day!'

Mel dug his elbow in Dodger's side. 'Those aren't the words!' he hissed.

'They're dashed good words. Better than your preachy stuff.' Dodger turned his attention to the face in the doorway who appeared to find their discussion very entertaining. 'My dear sir, would it please you to allow two young carol singers, come direct from St Paul's cathedral where we've been entertaining the honourable Lord Mayor himself, to share our songs with you on this festive eve with only the humblest hope of remuneration?' He jiggled his hat.

The man opened the door and slipped outside, casting a nervous look over his shoulder. He dropped a ha'penny in the hat. 'For my part I would gladly invite you in, but I'm only a clerk here.'

'Then might you ask Mr Marley if he would let us enter?' asked Mel.

The sash window next to the steps flew up. 'Bob Cratchit, what are you doing loitering on the step with those troublesome fellows?' bellowed a man, scowling from beneath grey bushy eyebrows. 'I told you to get rid of them. I suppose you'll think me unreasonable if I dock your pay for the time spent away from your desk?'

'I was just about to ask them to leave, sir,' replied Bob, waving frantically at the boys to get going.

'No matter, I'll tell them myself.' The man disappeared and then reappeared at the end of the corridor carrying a single candle.

Another person came out from the doorway opposite him, also carrying a light but with the addition that in his other hand he held a ruler. 'I'll send them about their ways, Ebenezer, don't you worry. A whack around the head should knock some sense into them.'

'Mr Marley!' cried Mel.

The ruler carrier came to the doorway, shouldering aside the clerk. 'Of course, I'm Mr Marley, young whippersnapper, who else would I be?' He slapped the ruler against the name on the sign like a schoolmaster pointing out the ABC on the blackboard.

'I recognize you – but you, you look different!' said Mel. Mr Marley had colour in his cheeks; not much admittedly, but enough that Mel knew this was no insubstantial body to be walked through but rather the man himself, still alive. One thing was different, however. 'Where are your chains and your cashboxes?'

Marley scowled down the length of his formidable nose. 'Cashboxes? What impertinence! How dare you ask me!'

His partner arrived at his side. Though the two men were very different in physique, Marley much taller and less bent over than his friend, they shared a similar cast of expression: secretive, suspicious, and, most of all, decidedly unfriendly.

'What's that he said?' asked Scrooge.

'He asked where we kept the money. I'm calling the watch.' Marley looked over Mel's head, ready to summon a constable.

'It is outrageous how even boys believe they have a right to steal from honest men at Christmas!' said Scrooge. 'You would sing me a song and put your hand right in my pocket to take the coin I've earned by hard labour, would you?'

Dodger looked very much as if that was exactly what he had in mind.

'No!' protested Mel. 'We just wanted to sing a carol and . . .' With a sinking heart he recognized that his slight chance of finding help with an old friend was fast disappearing. It might be hopeless to appeal to this Jacob Marley but he had to try. 'And ask for help for old times' sake.'

'Old times' sake?' scoffed Marley. 'Just because it is Christmas, doesn't mean I've taken leave of my senses. If you are in want of shelter, go to the union workhouse. That's what it's for. If you try to take anything from me, then you'll go to the prison. That's what that's for. Now get off our doorstep!'

'Yes, get away! And take your merry gentlemen with you!' seconded Scrooge.

Mel noticed, to his dismay, that the Dodger did not seem at all surprised by the outcome of this interview. He tipped his hat. 'God bless us, everyone!' he called happily, jumping down the steps and scooping snow off the railing. Spinning round, he threw the snowball, hitting Scrooge in the chest. 'Even you, you miserable old misers!' Laughing, he ran off. Mel followed hard on his heels, not waiting to find out how the missile had been received.

Round the corner and out of sight, the Dodger stopped by a wall to regain his breath. 'Oh my days, that was fun!'

Mel kicked a rut of compacted ice. 'You knew what Marley was like, didn't you?'

'Scrooge and Marley: the two most famously tight-fisted men in the city of London. And you wanted to go to them for help! That was a fine joke, that was.'

'I'm glad you find it funny but it means I'm back to square one.' Mel recalled too late how Mr Marley had told him he had to haunt the streets each night in payment for the chances to be kind that he had missed in life.

'I thought you said you had lots of friends.' Dodger tucked his thumbs back in his pockets.

'I do.' *Just not in this era.*

'Then ask one of them to help you.'

He hurried after his new friend. 'Dodger, where would you go to find someone to mend a special kind of clock?'

Dodger filched an orange from a rich lady's basket. 'What kind of clock?' He seemed interested by the question. He rolled the orange down his inner arm and flipped it up with a flex of his elbow before offering half of it to Mel. 'Grandfather or grandmother? Carriage or mantel? French, Swiss or London made?'

'London made.' That much Mel could guess. 'But it's not your usual kind. It's scientific. For experiments.'

'Then it's obvious. There are two places. Either you go to the men over at Greenwich who keep the clocks for the navy, or you go to those chaps at the Royal Institute who do the flash-bang experiments for the public.'

'Greenwich or the Royal Institute? Which is nearer?'

'Institute.' Dodger nodded. 'Come on, I'll take you there. They have meetings at Christmas. Would you believe it but people go and listen to some cove rumble on about chemistry and such?'

Mel hoped the Dodger was being so helpful because he wanted to make up for playing the trick about Marley, but he was beginning to have his doubts about his new friend. 'How do you know about this?'

Dodger tapped his nose. 'I make it my business to know everything that goes on in my city. And besides, an interested audience don't notice quick fingers slipping into back pockets, do they?'

The two boys made their way rapidly across town to Albemarle Street, pausing only to exchange a flurry of snowballs with some market boys at Covent Garden, and arrived in the West End outside a biscuit-coloured building with pillared facade. It looked the kind of place that only the very privileged would visit, not street children like Dodger.

'They let you in here?' asked Mel.

'Not as such,' admitted Dodger. 'I mingle with the crowd as they go in and out, getting an education at arm's length, you might say.'

The length was probably measured by the dip of a hand into an unguarded handbag.

Mel tried the door but it was locked. Peering through the windows, he could see a grand entrance hall with a white staircase splitting in two to lead to the upper floor. 'It's no good. No one's there. Maybe we should try Greenwich.'

Dodger tapped his shoulder. 'Weren't you asking me about a Faradiddle this morning?'

'I was.'

A name peeped out of the snow half covering the glass pane of a noticeboard. Dodger brushed the rest off. 'Well, I don't know him but here's another with a name in the same vein.'

Mel read the poster with growing excitement: 'A course of elementary lectures on electricity will be delivered during the Christmas vacation by Mr Faraday! That's the man!' Mel did a little victory jig on the spot.

'Am I brilliant or what?'

'You're brilliant – no question!'

Dodger grinned. 'You've got to come back later though. The lectures don't start till Tuesday.'

Mel read the remainder of the notice. 'The lectures will commence on the hour of three. Young children, ten shillings and sixpence.'

'Blimey, learning ain't cheap. They're on to a right good game here if they can charge people that much just to hear some stuffed shirt run on about things you'll never have any use for at home.' Dodger found a new reason to admire the men of the Royal Institute and tipped his hat to them.

Mel murmured his agreement but really he was thinking about his new goal. He had to gain enough money to buy a ticket on Tuesday and meet the scientist. But ten shillings and sixpence? Where on earth would he get so much and so quickly? He glanced at the Dodger, who was now studying the wipes he had filched on his way across town, picking at the embroidered initials on the corners. Stealing was only excusable as the last resort of the desperate – but Mel felt he had reached the point marked Pretty Desperate, having passed through the stages of Shock and Panic since being ripped out of his time. It looked like a dip into a life of crime beckoned.

Chapter Nine
Faraday's Riddle

After abandoning Mel to the three thugs, Krook made his way through the city without sparing a thought for the boy he left behind. Poor Lady Jane! He doubted that the men the Inventor had parked in his house would think to feed his cat while they held her hostage and, if he couldn't return in the next few days of her time, she might starve. He had to get time travelling again. He had to find someone who could help mend the time machine.

It took Krook the best part of two hours to limp and slide across London. He knew where he was going and was well prepared for this era, always carrying gold rather than worthless bank notes from the future. He congratulated himself on having signed up to all the major gentlemen's clubs in London early on in his explorations of the past. These institutions barely changed over the centuries and he could even ensure a familiar room was prepared for him when he turned up unannounced on their doorstep, a wing chair be waiting for him by a fireside, a good meal cooked by top chefs, and no questions asked. All that this had required was a quick visit to their members' records at regular intervals through the years, ticking off his name as having paid up the fee. He had even had the portrait of himself done as a fictitious ancestor for the walls of a couple of his favourites.

The Athenaeum was his pick for this visit, as he knew that the scientific gentlemen from the Royal Institute used it on a regular basis, thanks to its position close to Albemarle Street.

'Faradiddle? Farabibble? Fara-dee?' However hard Krook tried to call up the name of the genius who was widely recognized later in the century to have discovered how to apply electricity to practical uses, he could not quite capture it right. The man would be world-famous in a few years, but would he be so well known now? Making a little detour to Regent Street, Krook entered a tailor's shop as the assistant was just taking down the shutters ready for the first customer of the day.

'I want a suit of gentleman's clothes – sober but fashionable. Ready-made.'

The assistant looked down his thin nose at the windswept stranger in his tweed jacket cut far too short to be in vogue in this decade. Krook wore the thick wool for warmth as time travel was a chilly business. 'I'm afraid, sir, we don't carry off-the-peg items. If sir would like to visit the second-hand clothes stalls in Cheapside he might find what he was looking for.' The assistant appeared quite pleased with himself for this insult.

Krook had come across this attitude in 1815 and 1895 and, come to think of it, all dates between, and knew how to handle snobs. He slapped a small gold ingot on the counter. 'What do you say now, sonny?'

The assistant melted with greed. 'I apologize, sir. I have just remembered that we do have a set of clothes made for another client that might suit you. Sir Leicester Dedlock is about your size and rarely remembers to pay his bills so . . . well, he won't mind waiting.'

Krook was ushered into a velvet-curtained changing room, plied with tea and fresh baked buns, before emerging on to the street with attire and accessories appropriate to his era. He arrived on the doorstep of the Athenaeum Club in time for the morning papers, one of the busiest hours in the reading room. Leaving his old clothes in his favourite bedchamber at the back of the club, he joined the throngs of gentlemen sitting in leather-upholstered armchairs, faces hidden behind white paper walls. Krook didn't have a genteel air but had learned that as long as he passed himself off as an eccentric man of science he was accepted in this room.

'Mr Krook,' said the head waiter, 'we haven't seen you for a year or two but I never forget a face. Up from the country for a visit again?'

The problem with time travel was that Krook had no idea in which order he had visited the reading room. Two years ago could have been his first or tenth visit. He replied with a vague nod. 'That's right, Perkins.'

'Coffee and *The Times* wasn't it, sir?'

'That would be just the thing. Cold morning.'

'Yes, the weather is most inclement. Where will you be sitting?'

'I was wondering, if Mr Fara–' he hid the last syllable in a cough, 'was expected in?'

'Mr Faraday? Indeed, he is already here. I believe you'll find him in the library.'

'I've not had the pleasure of meeting him before. Could you take a note to him from me?'

'Of course, sir.'

Krook went to a writing table and scrawled a quick message.

> *I've something extraordinary of a scientific nature to show you.*
>
> *Yours, P Krook.*

Sipping his coffee, Krook watched as the waiter took his note on a silver salver to a man with a mass of dark curls sitting surrounded by bound volumes of the scientific papers. The man took the letter without reading it, so intent was he on finishing his sentence.

Finally, putting his pen aside, the scientist shook out the paper and read the message, his eyebrows winging up in surprise. He scanned the members in the reading room. Krook, in a rather embarrassed gesture, raised his hand to admit to being the sender. Faraday did not look encouraged to put a face to the note-writer but, nonetheless, good manners prevailed and he crossed the room to offer his hand to Krook.

'Good morning, sir. I'm Michael Faraday. I believe you have something you would like to show me?'

Krook had purchased a maroon gentleman's valise in a shop next door to the same tailor who had outfitted him. He produced it now. 'It is in here, sir. A most delicate object.'

Taking the vacant armchair opposite Krook, Faraday carefully removed the time machine with the skill of a man used to handling combustible materials. 'A clock?'

'Much more than a clock, sir.'

The scientist opened the door to examine the insides. 'By the great Galvani, this is indeed extraordinary!'

Krook had known it was a risk showing the machine to an expert but what else could he do? 'Do you know what it does?' he asked.

'I would guess that it is a very powerful electrical motor of some kind, but the workings are so tiny. Swiss watchmakers must have engineered this – I can barely make out the interlocking parts. But yes, yes, I think the principle is clear: that is the circuit, and this the magnet – but I've never seen one like this before. What is it made of? It is quite a riddle you've presented me. I fear to examine it closer in case I break it.'

'It's already broken. Do you know what went wrong?' asked Krook, pleased that Faraday had not pressed him with questions on the uses of the machine.

'It looks like there was some kind of blown-glass receptacle here. Maybe it held an illuminating element? There have been ideas that electricity could be used to create light. What is certain is that your circuit is blown. You overloaded the machine with a current it could not hold. See this here?' Faraday pointed to a coil of wire. 'This looks like a very advanced form of a voltaic pile. I thought I was doing the most progressive work in this field but it looks like someone is ahead of me. Where did you get this from?'

Krook was tempted to say it was his own invention but knew that under the briefest cross-examination from Faraday his ignorance would be obvious. 'I inherited it, from a scientifically minded uncle.'

'This is indeed very exciting – the best Christmas present I can imagine. Would you mind if I explored it further?'

Krook had already vowed not to let the time machine out of his sight. 'I'm afraid my first concern is to get it mended. I would be very happy to allow you to examine it once it is running again.' Not that he would still be here to let the scientist to do so.

Reluctantly, Faraday handed the time machine back. 'Then I suggest we manufacture a part to complete the circuit. I can do it myself if you let me take measurements now.'

'But of course! Thank you, sir.'

'However, I should warn you that you'll still need a replacement source of energy as yours is quite ruined. The Institute has the largest battery in existence. If you allow me, I can hook it up and see if we can get it running once more. What did you say it did again?'

'It measures things,' Krook said vaguely. 'It is best explained when I can demonstrate its uses to you.'

'Excellent. I'll look forward to that. Perhaps we can meet in my laboratory on Tuesday?' Faraday thumped his forehead. 'Silly! Of course, not Tuesday. I have a lecture to deliver. Let us meet Monday. I will have been able to come up with something by then, I'm sure, despite the Christmas holiday. Allow me take a few measurements and then we will be in business.'

Krook passed a comfortable Christmas as almost the sole person in the club apart from an elderly bishop who slumped most of the day in a chair in the library, either asleep or dead, Krook did not wish to enquire. The staff kept a fire in Krook's room, ensured he had a good dinner of goose and plum pudding, and filled his glass whenever it threatened to stand empty. Occasionally, he would look to the window and see snow falling and his thoughts would briefly touch on the boy he had abandoned on the Inventor's orders. He wondered if Melchizedek Foster was still alive. Still the boy was just an ordinary urchin, no parents, a few odd monster friends, no one who counted. Krook decided he should worry more about Lady Jane – that was a cat worth saving. He had to get back before he was missed.

A note arrived on Monday morning inviting Krook to attend Mr Faraday in the scientist's laboratory in the Royal Institute. Fortifying himself for a renewed bout of time travel, Krook polished off a modest breakfast of eggs, bacon, kippers, porridge and toast. Pleasantly full and eager to get back to his cat, he presented himself at the appointed hour at a side entrance to the Institute and was shown in to Mr Faraday's rooms. The laboratory was a spartan place – bare boards, white walls, floor-to-ceiling shelves stocked with chemical bottles. The lack of comforts did not matter to the occupant as the young scientist stood at a workbench, examining a glass bulb under a magnifying glass.

'Ah, Mr Krook. You have your machine with you?' said Faraday.

'Indeed, sir.' Wary of his ticket home being snatched from him, Krook put the time machine on the table. He had been trying not to think too much about what he would do if this failed. He had enough gold to live comfortably for a year or so but after that he would be thrown back into poverty – something his younger original self knew well in this time running a paltry rag and bottle shop. *If only I'd memorized the names of the Derby winners*, he thought glumly, realizing he had not made the most of the opportunities for personal enrichment his machine had given him.

Mr Faraday opened the machine with an air of reverence, a worshipper of technology treading holy ground. 'I've never seen such workmanship. If only one might invent a machine to make things so small, what could we not do with electricity! My electric rotor might then be possible. Who did you say made this?'

Krook muttered something about the imaginary uncle.

'Your uncle, Mr Krook, must have been a genius,' replied Faraday, caressing the gold casing. 'Did he leave any notes?'

'There might be some. I'll have to look, sir.'

'And is this the only machine of its kind?'

'At the moment, I would think so.' Krook chuckled inwardly at his private joke.

'So, to work. First we take out the old fixings and then we attach the glass bulb here and here.' Faraday bent over the open machine like a dentist doing a delicate tooth extraction. 'The man who made this was brilliant. I can't believe how strong he had made the mechanism. It looks fragile but I can see that it will withstand a great deal of stress. Then I'll touch the connector rods at either end. Let's see if I've completed the circuit.'

The glass tube lit up, casting a white light like magnesium burning.

'By George, you've done it!' Krook clapped his hands in delight. 'Just let me borrow this broom and strap it in place.'

Faraday scratched his head as his guest took the laboratory brush from its corner. 'Whatever do you need that for?'

'It works better on a pole. Trust me: I have some experience with this.' Krook settled the broom between his legs and set the dial to 1895. 'Right: what do I have to do make this run at full power?'

'This is most peculiar.'

'Just tell me!' Krook was losing his temper now. He didn't have to be nice to this man any longer; he would be away from him and never looking back in half a tick.

Faraday frowned disapprovingly at Krook's attack of bad manners. 'Well, I suppose, sir, that we must attach the ends to the Royal Institute battery. It is the most powerful one ever built and should provide you with enough electricity to restart your machine.' Faraday produced two clamps from under the table. 'These wires will connect it.' He glanced down at the wooden handle. 'It's a good job that your pole doesn't conduct electricity or you might find this very uncomfortable.'

'Don't worry about me. Let's get on with it.' Krook gripped the pole and braced himself for another flight through time.

Mel spent Christmas Day huddled by the fire in Fagin's tumbledown lodgings. The Dodger, much amused by their carol singing expedition, got him to perform a few more hymns for the thieves who had gathered there in retreat from the snow. Nancy showed she too must once have been a pew polisher for she joined in the choruses, la-la-ing where she couldn't recall the words. Mel began to feel almost at home, enjoying the laughter and appreciative applause of the thieves, though he was missing Eve desperately. Nancy was nice enough but she could never replace his best friend. He had bitten his nails to the quick worrying that Krook had already mended the time machine and flown off, leaving him behind forever. He didn't want to think about all the sad Christmases to come if he was stuck for good in this era.

The dinner was a sorry affair. Fagin had obtained a scrawny chicken for roasting. Nancy had filched three oranges. The Dodger had stolen some potatoes and a plum pudding, the latter big enough for a mouthful each.

'Barely worth the boiling, my dear,' said Fagin, wrapping the pudding in a muslin cloth to be placed in a pan of bubbling water.

'Do you want me to take it back then, Fagin?' asked Dodger, pretending to remove the pudding from the stove.

'No, my dear. You are very quick tonight, aren't you,

Dodger? I'm grateful, we're all most grateful that we have such a skilled obtainer of puddings among us.'

'I took it from the window sill of a family up Camden Town. Not my fault they couldn't feed a frog on what their old man earns.' Dodger sat down next to Mel on the low bench by the fire, the warmest spot in the room.

'Shouldn't you only steal from the rich?' suggested Mel, feeling guilty he'd eaten someone else's pudding.

'They're still better off than us, with a house and a regular wage coming in. And I would go out and look for richer baskets but there's no point.'

'Snow driven everyone inside?' asked Nancy, nibbling on a segment of orange to savour the pleasure. 'No one on the streets?'

'Not a living leg,' confirmed the Dodger.

'Tomorrow will be better. People out walking with their families, new clothes, new gloves, new wipes.'

'Yes, tomorrow will be a grand day for fogel-hunters.' The Dodger dug inside his pocket. 'I got this too. I thought you'd like it.' He put a little puppet on a pole in Nancy's lap. 'If you pull the string, the man jigs.'

Nancy duly followed his instructions, making the little man in green dance, arms and legs flying up. She laughed so hard tears poured from her eyes. Mel didn't think it was a happy laugh. 'Oh my, he looks like a man being scragged,' she declared.

Nancy was right: the little figure did look like a man hanging from the noose.

Fagin flinched and knocked it from her hand. 'Leave it out, Nance. Show some respect to poor Jim.'

She picked it out of the ashes on the hearth, wiped it on her apron, and gave it back to Dodger. 'He's right. You keep it.'

Trying to recapture a lighter mood, the Dodger grinned. 'So I will – to remind me what I've got to dodge. I'm not destined for the nipping jig, me. I'm going to retire a rich man and eat plum pudding every day.'

'Talking about avoiding things,' said Mel, 'I've stayed inside too long. I'd better come with you tomorrow.'

Dodger and Fagin exchanged a glance. 'Is he ready, do you think, my dear?' asked Fagin.

'What's the hurry, Doorstop?' asked Dodger. 'You in a rush to get caught by the traps?'

'I need to get into that lecture to see Mr Faraday. I have to earn the entry fee.'

Dodger pushed back the brim of his hat. 'My eyes, Mel, you are jolly green after all. You don't need to steal the entry fee; you just need to filch a ticket from someone's pocket! They'll all be fussing and squabbling like geese as they get out of their carriages. There'll be plenty of opportunities for two enterprising young gents to save the poor little rich children from an hour of education they don't want.'

Mel sighed with relief. One pickpocketing of a piece of paper in a very good cause he could forgive himself. He hadn't been sure that he would be able to go through with a stealing spree no matter how desperate he was. The main problem with theft was you were never sure how desperate your victim was. The stories of Robin Hood made it sound easy to steal from the rich to give to the poor. In London, it seemed it was more a case of steal from the poor to give to the dishonest.

The Dodger's thoughts had been running on a different track. 'I must say, Doorstop, you're right about one thing: you'll need to practise. Fagin, the wipes.'

'Ah yes, my dear, just the game for a holiday.' Fagin began planting a rainbow of handkerchiefs about his person. The ends dangled out making him resemble an odd form of Christmas tree, thanks to his frayed bottle-green dressing gown. 'Imagine me, an unsuspecting old gentleman, walking down the Strand, not a care in the world, unobservant of all around me as I admire my new togs in the windows – never forget the windows, Master Foster.'

Dodger started following the pacing Fagin, thumbs tucked in his lapels. 'Windows can be killers. Wait until there's a gap – a friendly alley or brick wall – then you can pass.' Increasing his speed, he overtook Fagin. A blue handkerchief had vanished from the right-hand pocket.

Fagin stopped and clapped his hand to his side. 'Oh my dears! The horror! I've been robbed most cruelly! My favourite wipe, embroidered by my sacred aunt, it's gone!' He pretended to sob into a white one, which he then replaced in the same pocket with a wink at Mel. 'Now it's your turn, young Mel.'

Mel had been watching very closely how the Dodger made his steal and where he had stowed his gains. Brushing past the Dodger to take his place behind Fagin, he slapped the boy's arm. 'That was smoothly done, Dodger.'

'Why thank you, Mel.' The Dodger preened, examining his quick fingers with professional delight. 'Let's see if you can do the same. Quick, no hesitations, that's how to do it.'

Mel mimicked Dodger's strut behind the strolling Fagin, making Nancy giggle.

'And now I begin again on my sad way, lamenting the loss of my Auntie Sarah's gift,' said Fagin. 'I pause to admire myself in a plate glass window and –'

Mel overtook him and bowed.

'You're supposed to wait until he's got past the window,' said Nancy helpfully.

Ignoring this commentary, Mel coughed. 'Dear sir, I heard your sorrow from the top of Ludgate Hill. Could it possibly be this wipe that you have lost?' He held out an identical blue handkerchief.

'What!' Dodger pushed a hand up his cuff.

'Oh my dear, it is!' cried Fagin. 'What a likely young lad you are, and so kind to have restored it to me. Have a sixpence for your trouble.' He mimed pressing the coin in Mel's palm.

'Oh no, sir. My reward is knowing I've done a good deed,' said Mel, feigning an angelic look and pushing the gift away, bowing all the while. 'Good day to you.'

Fagin returned the bow and then dropped his act. He span on the spot, clapping his hands in glee. 'You filched it from the Dodger, didn't you? I've never seen the like. Dodger, you have a rival!'

Grumpily, the Dodger squatted by the fire and gave it a rough poke. 'That's all very well, but he was supposed to lift a wipe, not hand one back.'

Mel sat beside him. 'Are you so sure I didn't?' He began removing handkerchiefs from up his sleeves. 'Right pocket, left pocket, breast pocket, waistcoat pocket. It's all in the bowing.'

Nancy gave a huff of laughter and drained her tankard of beer. 'He's a sharp one, this kid, Fagin. Send him out with the Dodger and all London will be going home in nothing but their shirts, and them only if they're inferior quality not worth the stealing.'

Fagin lifted the pudding out of the pan and unwrapped it, releasing a curl of fragrant steam. 'I think we can say training is done, my dears. Where did you learn to pick pockets, Master Foster? I'd like to send some of my boys to your school.'

'Here and there,' replied Mel. In fact, he had picked up some lessons in the orphanage from other street children and perfected his skills under Cain's tutelage. The Jekyll twins had been of the opinion that monsters were bound to run into trouble and might require sleight of hand to escape – a palmed key or removal of incriminating documents, all these they had foreseen. Stealing a ticket to get into a lecture given sixty years ago hadn't been on the curriculum but Mel guessed the principle was the same: in a world set against their sort, monsters did what they had to do to survive.

'Indeed, I often say that most of life's lessons are best gained "here and there",' continued Fagin, cutting the pudding into five parts. He placed two portions on each plate, reserving the third and solitary portion for the man who lived next door with Nancy. He put it on the stove to keep warm. He then gave the Dodger and Mel the same plate, angling the slice with a sprig of holly on top towards his current favourite. He pinched Mel's chin between forefinger and thumb. 'Keep your mysteries, young Mel, but don't keep your gains from me. You steal and I look after the goods, converting them into coin. That's how things work round here.'

'And remember who's the senior hand,' grumbled the Dodger, twisting the plate so he got the holly.

Mel let that go. 'I promise I won't forget, as long as I'm with you, that is.' He wondered how long that would be. He'd not yet spent a Christmas with Eve, the Jekylls and his other monster friends. Would they in the future be dining on plum pudding cooked by the mummy and thinking of him or would they have given up hope of ever seeing him back again?

Eve won't give up, he told himself. *And I won't give up trying to get to her, even if years pass before I succeed.*

Chapter Ten
Krook's Lair

As Quasimodo had described the thief's hideout to be near the river, the Jekyll twins organized for a police riverboat to take them downstream. It was a poignant journey for Eve: the first time she had been on the Thames was when she had arrived with Mel a few months ago. Everything had been new and strange but Mel had been on hand to explain it to her. Now she was watching Quasimodo be astonished by the number of ships below Tower Bridge. He stood at the boat's rail staring for some minutes, mouth open in wonder.

'Like nest of ants.' He mimed the scurrying motion of the insects, which did resemble the oars of the wherries and skiffs dipping in and out of the water

157

as they went from ship to shore, carrying passengers and cargo off smaller vessels. The big steamers and ocean-going ships were moored further downriver in the new docks, marked by the cranes bristling over the roofs of the Isle of Dogs, a set of canine whiskers.

Eve allowed Quasimodo space to marvel at the steamers, barges, sailing ships at anchor, then tugged him back to the business of locating the thief's hideout.

'So do you think it was near here that he lives?' she asked.

'All you have to do is take us somewhere close to the spot, sahib. Once we draw close, the wolves and I will take over,' said Mowgli, leaning on the rail next to Quasimodo. At the bow of the boat the pack clustered; wolfish eyes shone with a hungry glint as they watched fishing boats unload their catch at Billingsgate, crates mobbed by seagulls. Boys stood on hand to drive them off with stones. Cain and Abel were talking to the policeman at the wheel. They had swapped bodies before leaving the house. Despite carrying on a polite conversation, Cain swung his walking stick with a jerky motion, sign of his pent-up fury. Mel was his friend too, Eve reminded herself. Abel was fretting the cottons poking out of a frayed cuff, a rare sign of his unease. She found the activities of both brothers disheartening. Usually the twins could find a bright side in most situations; they had to be really pessimistic about the chances of getting Mel back to allow their bad humour to show.

No, she wasn't going to think like that. They were going to find the thief and save Mel. Eve Frankenstein did not lose hope. It was just a shame that Constable Wilkins hadn't been able to come with them. He was on duty in Scotland Yard and his sergeant had refused him permission to accompany them. Eve missed his cheerful face.

'Eve! There! There I was!' Quasimodo grabbed her arm. The boat had just rounded another bend taking them to Rotherhithe and he had spotted something on the bank. It was difficult to see the shore clearly, thanks to the cluster of vessels. Several of them were moored so that their bowsprits could have been used to hang the washing of the houses they nearly touched. Mariner and slum dweller could have talked ship-to-shore without raising their voices. Many of the buildings were built right on the brink of the water, propped up on logs, that it appeared it would only take a smashed bottle of champagne and a nudge to launch them upon the waves.

'What do you see, *mon petit*?' she asked.

'That house. Looks like hat.' Quasimodo was pointing to a stubby-looking building right on the end of a dirty terrace of cottages. It had the shape of an upside-down flowerpot.

'Are you sure?'

Quasimodo nodded. 'Bad man say it like me with lump on its back.'

That was a cruel observation but the building did indeed have a bulge on the top, probably once the hub around which windmill sails used to rotate.

'We should land there,' Eve called to the man at the wheel, pointing to a little shingle river beach below the house. 'Quasimodo thinks we've found it.'

The pilot in his peaked cap nosed the boat towards the bank. 'You'll have to get your feet wet for the last few yards, miss.'

Eve didn't wait for him to cut the engine. She splashed down into the water and carried the other passengers two at a time to the shore without stopping to ask permission; first Quasimodo and Mowgli, then the twins, then two of the river policemen, leaving only the pilot to guard the boat. The Thames smelt vile, a mixture of rubbish and mud, all the worse when her feet stirred it, but she didn't care. They were one step closer to saving Mel.

The wolves had opted to make the transfer under their own power, clearing the distance from the prow to dry ground with four impressive leaps one after the other. Mowgli led them up the slimy steps to street level, taking shelter in the doorway of a tavern from the steady drizzle that had begun to fall. There were faded red curtains dangling at the windows and a sign over the entrance declaring the very miserable building was in fact called the *Six Jolly Fellowship-Porters*, the inn favoured by the boatmen.

'My brothers, do you have the scent?' asked Mowgli.

The wolves lifted their snouts in the air, sampling whatever came to them on the breeze. Grey Wolf let out a long howl that rose and fell eerily. Doors banged and shutters closed as the locals reacted to the unexpected presence of monsters and a pack of wolves among them.

'We don't serve your sort!' shouted a woman from an upstairs window of the tavern.

Ignoring this discourtesy, Mowgli turned to Eve. 'Good news, my sister. The wolves say that the stench of time hangs heavy in the air. They say it is most like the smoke of funeral pyres on the banks of the Ganges, time past and time present mixed. We have come to the right place.'

'And does it originate in that old windmill?' asked Cain.

With a flick of a hand held up to his ear, Mowgli sent the youngest wolf to explore. Little Akela wove himself into the shadows, barely visible even to those watchers who knew he was there. He slunk around the perimeter of the building, paying particular attention to the door at the front. He disappeared from view on the far side but soon returned carrying a fish skeleton. It drooped from his mouth like a walrus moustache. He let it fall at Mowgli's sandalled feet, then sat down on his haunches to make his report, wagging tail wiping an arc in the mud clear to the cobblestones. Mowgli nodded and yipped once, then scratched the wolf behind the ears.

'Little Akela says that the smell is strongest inside the house. It is not empty. He found a cat locked in an outhouse. There is at least one person inside. The time traveller is not working alone.'

Eve wished with all her heart that the time traveller had returned so they could wring Mel's location out of him. That would make a rescue so much more possible.

Cain and Abel conferred quickly. 'Mowgli, we must not let anyone escape the house,' said Cain. 'We must trap the time traveller – and the Inventor too if he is here. Please ask your wolves to guard all exits including the windows. We'll need someone underneath the house too in case there's a trapdoor to the river.'

Mowgli nodded, sending the wolves off to patrol the territory Cain had marked out.

'Mademoiselle Eve and I will go through the front door. Abel and the policemen will take the back.'

'What about Quasimodo?' asked Eve.

'Oh yes.' Cain cast a concerned look at the boy. Though Quasimodo was big, they had no idea yet how he would do in a battle. So far he had shown only reluctance to harm anyone unless he was in a panic, but he couldn't be left alone on the streets. 'He should come with us too, but tell him he has to stay out of the way if it comes to blows.'

162

Eve was confident she could handle any fighting that needed doing. She explained the situation in simple words so that Quasimodo did not lose his head if a battle broke out.

'Everyone clear on their part in this plan?' asked Cain.

The monsters and policemen nodded.

'Then good luck, friends. Remember: no one must get away. Speed is of the essence. We must get inside and stop anyone using a time machine to escape.'

'And what's our signal, brother?' asked Abel.

Cain gave him a wicked little smile, taking a revolver out of his coat pocket. 'When the wolf howls, we attack.'

It was fifteen minutes before the start of the lecture and the carriages were arriving. Stomach empty, hands and face grubby as there was no pump near Fagin's lodgings, feet sore from so much walking, Mel watched from behind a parked hansom cab as rich young ladies and gentlemen got out of their barouches, cabriolets and phaetons, drawn by exquisite horses that doubtless had been better stabled and fed over the last few days than him. Some families who lived nearby were arriving on foot, umbrellas held over flowered bonnets and top hats.

Dodger nudged Mel. 'See that boy in the blue breeches and black coat, the one who just kicked the girl?'

'I see them.' The girl had just elbowed what Mel took to be her brother, but she had been spotted by the governess and was now receiving a lecture on ladylike manners. The rest of the party included another sister in fine clothes, a quiet little girl in a grey wool dress who stood to one side, and what had to be the boy's flamboyantly dressed mother.

'He's a prime plant – if he wants to go to the lecture, then I'm the Archbishop of Canterbury. See, he's got his ticket sticking out of his coat pocket, just begging for it to fall out or be taken.' Dodger gave Mel a quick inspection. 'You look more like a servant than a rich boy. When you go in, if anyone asks, say you're holding a place for your master. They won't doubt that story.'

'Thanks, Dodger. Where will you wait for me?'

Dodger scratched his nose, eyes shifting up and down the street. 'How long will you be?'

'A couple of hours, I guess.'

'I'll come back then. I've got business at Westminster Abbey. There's a carol service on this afternoon and you've given me a taste for such things. First, I'll give you a hand here. You circle round and I'll get his attention with a snowball.'

With a salute, Mel crossed the street and walked up fifty yards to approach the entrance to the Royal Institute from the north. Just as he came shoulder to shoulder with the boy they had picked out, a snowball came out of nowhere and hit the young gentleman in the face.

'Aaah!' shrieked the boy, staggering back into Mel. The ticket swiftly transferred to a new pocket. 'Oooh! Ow! Who did that?'

At first Mel thought the Dodger's target was making a lot of fuss about nothing until he saw that the boy had a cut on his brow. There must've been a stone caught up in the compacted snow.

'That looks nasty. May I lend you a handkerchief?' Mel pulled out a blue wipe that he had kept as trophy from the game.

'Get away from me, you nasty little creature!' The boy pushed him away. 'Mama, my eye, it's bleeding. I'll go blind!'

'John Reed, behave yourself, you're in public,' hissed his mother, snatching the handkerchief from Mel's outstretched hand without a word of thanks.

Relieved the Dodger had selected such a repulsive specimen of their own age on whom it was not worth wasting an ounce of regret, Mel slid further up the line and through the front doors with a wave of the ticket. He wasn't going to take the place specified on the voucher – that would give him away when the rest of the Reed family took their places – but it had got him through the doors, which had been his aim. Now all he needed was a quiet word with Mr Faraday. Wriggling like an eel through the brightly coloured shoal of guests come to the gawp at the spectacle in the auditorium, Mel found a door at the far side, tucked behind a white statue of a man only half dressed, Greek robes falling off one shoulder. He tried the handle and peeked in on a dull corridor and steep staircase behind. Excellent: this had to be the servants' domain, just what he needed. He stepped through, acting as if he had every right to be there, and closed the door on the hubbub behind.

Having lived with the Jekylls, Mel had experience of men of a scientific bent. He knew that though they may have posh rooms out front for visitors, the real work got done in laboratories stripped of anything that could get damaged. Mr Faraday would have somewhere like that in the building, he was sure of it. He also knew the man was due in the lecture theatre in ten minutes so he would be here, preparing for the talk. Where better than in his private rooms? The corridor led Mel around the outside of the auditorium and to the back of the Institute. Footmen hurried to and from the kitchens, not sparing a glance for the stranger in their midst. It looked like the Institute had hired in extra hands to serve refreshments to the biggest crowd in its calendar of events so a new face was unremarkable. Taking the opposite direction to the busy kitchens Mel opened a few doors until he found one leading on to a quiet room and what he had been looking for.

'Yes? Is it time to begin?' A dark-haired gentleman, younger than Mel expected, looked up from a sheaf of notes he had spread out on a workbench.

'Mr Faraday?'

'Of course. You haven't come to fetch me then?' The man took a sip from a cup of tea. 'Ugh, cold. I'm afraid I haven't time if you are after a job. My laboratory boy did leave in a hurry after that unfortunate accident with the wet battery and there is a vacancy but I can't talk about that now. Come back after the lecture.'

'It's not about a job, sir. It's about a time machine.'

Faraday gathered his papers together then tapped them straight. 'A what?'

'A machine that travels through time.'

'That's what I thought you said. Well, sorry, lad, but such things are impossible. I haven't got time for a fairy story, inventive though your approach is to gaining my attention. I have several hundred people waiting to hear about electricity.'

Mel felt desperate. He had to do something to get this man's serious notice. 'Sir, you like electricity? Well then, I'll show you electricity.' Spotting a glass bell jar standing on a side table, he placed his hands flat against the sides and sent a little of his power into the vessel. Blue rays of a miniature lightning storm sparked and jagged inside.

'What the blazes is that?' cried Faraday. He put his hand on the glass and some of the rays danced towards him so the storm was split three ways. 'You've made a Leyden jar – but it's not connected to anything! What's happening? Do you have some special form of animal magnetism . . . but no, no, I've concluded that all electricity is essentially the same thing. Can you stop it?'

Mel withdrew his power from the glass and the storm snuffed out.

'By Volta, that is remarkable. This certainly has been a week for marvels!' Faraday quite forgot that he should ask permission. He grabbed Mel's wrist and took his pulse. 'A little elevated.' He felt his forehead. 'Warm but not feverish. How did you do it?'

There was a knock at the door. Opening it halfway, a ginger-haired gentleman put his head around the edge. 'Sir, the audience is seated. We're ready for you.'

'Coming, Jarvis. Blasted lecture.' He tucked his notes into a leather folder. 'You'll remain here till I've finished?'

Mel wasn't sure that was wise. He did not want to become an experiment. He'd come for answers.

Faraday must have read his doubt from his expression. 'Better still, you can come with me. With my assistant gone, I need someone to pass me things. Just don't muck up my demonstration with that . . . that thing you do.'

'But, sir . . .'

'I'll pay you.'

Now he was talking! Mel was tired of the guilt that he was living off a gang of thieves, and he was also very hungry. A few honestly earned shillings would be very welcome. 'All right, I'll stay. Thank you.'

'What's your name, boy?'

'Melchizedek Foster.'

Faraday smiled. 'Really? After the Old Testament king? A bit of a mouthful for a small boy.'

'People call me Mel.'

'Well then, Mel, we'd better get going before they send someone else to drag us out of here.'

Mel decided he liked Mr Faraday. He showed no airs and graces, talking to Mel as an equal. He reminded Mel of Cain who, though he was a young gentleman born and bred, never treated Mel as a common working boy, which is exactly what he had been before joining the monsters. How he missed his friends.

'Do you know the names of the basic scientific equipment used in electricity?' asked Faraday, showing Mel up some stairs leading to the stage area in the auditorium.

Mel had helped the twins in their experiments often enough. 'Yes, sir.'

'Oh? You've worked for a scientist before? That's good. We must talk more about this after the lecture. I can see I might have found myself a new laboratory boy.' Faraday opened one of a pair of double doors and stepped out on to the brightly lit stage. A ripple of applause greeted his entrance. Mel followed him and stood to one side where he hoped he would attract the least attention. He could see rows of people, including near the front the boy that had been struck by the

Dodger's snowball. His mother must have talked his way in for him without a ticket, a fact that the boy did not appear to be enjoying. He was currently amusing himself by pulling the hair of the girl in grey beside him and then looking innocent when she turned round to complain.

'Ladies and gentlemen, thank you for coming today.' Mr Faraday began a clear and very amusing account of the discovery of electricity, from the early speculation about lightning to the more recent invention of batteries to store the power.

'And here is a most remarkable object.' Mel's heart missed a beat when Mr Faraday held up the key Benjamin Franklin had used to capture lightning when kite-flying in a thunderstorm – not because the key was a great scientific relic, which indeed it was, but because he knew that object very personally, or would do fifty years later when he was born. His father had acquired it and Mel's mother had put it round his neck immediately after his birth. Being struck by lightning had left Mel with a key-shaped scorch mark on his chest and his weird ability to act as a conductor of electricity. Here it was again at an earlier point in its story. The spiralling circles in history caused by time travel made Mel's brain ache.

Mr Faraday turned round and handed Mel the key to put back on the equipment table. Was it his imagination, or was the key humming like a tuning fork in his hand? He put it down and gave it an affectionate pat. He wouldn't move it again from its intended spot in case he did something to stop his own powers forming all those years into the future.

'And now I'd like a volunteer to help me with this next experiment,' said Mr Faraday, looking out at the ranks of people watching him. 'How about you, young lady?' His gaze had fallen on the girl sitting next to the objectionable boy. A round face with a little pointy chin, grey eyes, hair scraped back, she looked intelligent and had clearly been following every word of the lecture.

'Me, sir?' she asked, pressing her fingers to her chest to check he had indicated the correct person.

'Yes, you, young lady. What's your name?'

'Jane Eyre, sir.'

'Well, Miss Eyre, please come down. This won't hurt, I promise.' Mr Faraday gave her a friendly smile.

The girl rose, blushing slightly. Mel noticed that none of the rest of the girl's party looked very pleased to see her singled out. As she tried to pass John Reed, he did not move his knees and, Mel suspected, tripped her on purpose. Jane fell heavily on her palms and knees into the gangway while the boy sniggered. She would have bruises later.

'Jane, you are making a spectacle of yourself!' snapped the boy's mother who sat with her two girls in the row in front. 'Mr Faraday, you should choose a better assistant. One of my daughters perhaps?'

With a defiant toss of her head, Jane stood up. 'No, Aunt Reed, I agreed to do it and I shall keep my word.'

Like a little soldier marching into battle, she stomped down the stairs and joined Mr Faraday and Mel on the stage.

'Hold this end of the circuit, Miss Eyre,' said Mr Faraday, handing her a copper loop that ran back to a battery. 'I'm going to demonstrate a trick that was all the rage at parties a hundred years ago. I want you to hold hands with me, I'll hold hands with – oh, and we need another to complete the circuit. Any volunteers?'

The objectionable boy's hand shot up among many others. An idea came to Mel.

'Choose that boy in blue,' murmured Mel so only Mr Faraday heard.

'Are you sure? He looks an unpleasant sort,' he whispered back.

'Trust me, he deserves it.'

'And you, sir, we'll take you,' said Mr Faraday out loud. A smattering of applause followed John Reed as he bounded down the steps. He made sure he accidentally-on-purpose jostled Jane as he passed and ignored Mel altogether as beneath his notice. Mel could see that Jane looked disappointed to have her special moment shared with her companion.

Mr Faraday held out his palm. 'Young sir, if you would hold my hand.'

'I'll take that place, if you don't mind,' said Mel

quickly. He slipped in between the two. The ring was complete. Jane held the copper and Mr Faraday's hand; Mel held Mr Faraday's and John Reed's hands; John Reed held the copper loop leading back to the battery.

'Everyone ready?' asked Mr Faraday. 'Miss Eyre, if you would just touch that loop to the red knob on the top of the battery and . . . feel that, everyone?'

Jane laughed. 'Yes! It's a tingle, like a cat purring inside you.'

'We can all feel it as the electricity passes from body to body. You must only do this with very low voltages, of course, as higher ones risk giving you a shock, so please, do not try this at home.'

'I don't like it!' squealed John Reed. His hair was rising from his scalp to stand up on end.

'Be a man, boy!' said Mr Faraday. 'Look, the little lady isn't making any fuss.'

Mel smiled. He had been boosting the current as it passed through him, giving John Reed a stronger dose, enough to feel like painful pins and needles in his arm. Time to end the show. He released a controlled burst, the equivalent of a stinging slap, and John dropped his end of the chain.

'Ow! Mama, Mama, the nasty man lied! That hurt!' John burst into noisy sobs.

Mr Faraday's dark eyes flashed at the accusation of lying. 'The only way the current could reach you was through us and none of us felt anything of the sort.'

173

He turned to the audience. 'Ma'am, I don't know what kind of milksop you are raising, but he clearly isn't suited to the serious pursuit of science. I suggest you remove him immediately.'

Mrs Reed swept down the steps and collected her son, who was still shaking his wrist. 'Come on, precious. I will not stay to be insulted. I'll take you for an ice at Gunter's, lambkin.'

'Get off!' moaned John as she smoothed his sticky-up hair.

'You did something, didn't you?' whispered Jane to Mel under the cover of the commotion John Reed created being towed from the hall.

'I might've done a little something. Is he always this horrid?'

'This is one of his better days,' she replied darkly.

There was much muttering in criticism of the over-indulgent mother as Mrs Reed and John departed. Jane returned to her seat with a shy smile at Mel and sat down behind the two girls in their party who had elected to stay with their governess. They seemed quite pleased to see the back of their brother. Mr Faraday went on to repeat the experiment with other members of the audience, this time not involving Mel, so all went smoothly.

'And that concludes today's lecture,' Mr Faraday announced. 'Tomorrow I will tell you about the dangerous experiments of Herr Doctor Frankenstein on the human body and the limits of scientific exploration.'

The audience applauded and Mr Faraday took a bow. 'Come, Mel, you owe me an explanation,' he said, taking Mel's elbow and steering him out.

'What's that about Frankenstein, sir?' asked Mel. He felt he knew quite a lot about that man's experiments thanks to his own close-up experience of awakening Eve. She had described Frankenstein as her making grandfather.

'Don't sidetrack me, Mel. I want you to explain how you made that boy wince when the voltage on that battery wasn't even enough to make a frog's legs twitch.'

'Ah.'

'Yes, ah.' Faraday opened the door to his laboratory, pausing only briefly to acknowledge the band of well-wishers and autograph hunters who had come behind the stage to greet him. Once they crossed the threshold, he closed the door and shot the bolt. 'How did you do it?'

'He deserved it. He made that girl fall over, you do realize that?'

'I didn't say "why" but "how". I quite agree that the little toad was a poisonous example of the male of the species so I am not cross that you did that, even if you did risk my professional reputation. Come on, spill your secrets.'

Mel shrugged. 'I'm a sort of electricity-powered

monster.' He paused, wondering how much Faraday could take. 'From the future.'

Faraday pulled off his necktie, clearly having decided that one did not need to be formally dressed in the presence of an electric monster. 'Your body acts as some kind of battery? A storage device?'

'I'm not sure. The power doesn't seem to run out.'

'So you generate electricity too. Fascinating. Do you want a biscuit?' Faraday went to a series of jars marked with names like Arsenic and Lead. Mel was pretty sure a biscuit laced with either would kill him. Faraday picked the Arsenic one and held it out, shaking his head and smiling when he saw Mel's expression. 'Don't worry: I only keep my biscuits in here because my fellow scientists are terrible thieves. This jar has never had arsenic in, I promise. I'm rather good at chemistry too, you know, so I'm sure.'

Mel wasn't at all certain it was wise but took a biscuit. It looked innocent enough – sugar coated with a rich golden crumb – and he was extremely hungry. Faraday selected one for himself and munched on it while clearing a space on his cluttered workbench. He pulled out a stool for each of them to sit on.

'That's better. You've shown me that you do indeed in some mysterious way store an unusual amount of electricity in your body. Now explain this claim to have come from the future.'

Mel finished his biscuit. 'I know it sounds farfetched

but I was brought here unwillingly from, well . . . 1895.'

'Indeed. And what's the world like in 1895?' Faraday sounded amused and sceptical.

'It's . . .' Mel paused. If he said too much would he risk changing the future? Cain had said he felt the present was too robust to worry about what might have happened in the past but could he put his trust in that? He could do something that would prevent him ever returning home. What if something he said changed the course of Faraday's life? The man was clearly on the path to being a notable scientist. An alteration in his career was exactly the kind of event that would shift the sequence off their current track. 'It's pretty much like now.'

'Oh, you aren't spinning me a very good story, Mel.' Faraday looked disappointed.

Mel realized that he was facing a man who might understand the position he found himself in. Honesty was his best chance of getting help. 'Actually, I'm not spinning any tale because of the time paradox.'

Faraday brushed the edge of his jaw with a forefinger, then tapped his lips. 'Which means you don't want to tell me anything that might change history. Clever. You've found an argument that almost makes me believe in you. Have another biscuit.'

Mel took one with a chocolate glaze this time. After the scarce fare in Fagin's lodgings, this tasted wonderful. 'I suppose it isn't really important if you believe me or not as I'm really here to ask you if you've met an odd man recently.'

'Yes,' said Faraday with a twinkle in his eye. 'A young one – and I'm eating biscuits with him.'

Mel smiled. 'Besides me. He has grey hair, appears to be about sixty, was wearing a tweed suit when I last saw him, and he has a machine that looks like a gold clock.'

On this last piece of information, Faraday forgot his biscuit. 'You know Mr Krook?'

'So that's his name! Yes, he brought me here from the future. Have you seen him?'

'Yes, indeed, in this very room. I saw him yesterday. I mended his machine for him.'

'Where is he? I can't tell you how important it is that I find him! The time machine is my only ticket home.'

Faraday shook his head, not really listening to Mel as he was still thinking about the mechanism he had helped repair. 'A time machine? I suppose it is theoretically possible if the technology came from the future. We can't come close to anything of the sort in our era.'

'Please, sir, where is he?'

'That fellow Krook?'

Mel nodded.

'I'm sorry, Mel, but he's gone.'

Chapter Eleven

A Krooked House

'We're looking for an old man who smells of time, remember. On the count of three.' Back against the crumbling mill wall, Cain held up his fingers so Grey Wolf could see the countdown with his sharp eyes from across the road. 'One, two, three!'

A wolf howl rose up to the sullen skies.

Eve kicked the door. It flew off its hinges, flattening the man in the room beyond who had come to investigate the noise. She ducked in to the left, Quasimodo following her; Cain went to the right, his revolver covering the room.

'Stay where you are!' he warned a second man who had risen from his place at the table near the kitchen fire, a dog barking at his heels. 'Where's the time traveller?'

The man dived for the rear exit, running straight

into Abel who grabbed him in a headlock before he could shout for help.

'Eve, upstairs!' said Cain.

Eve bounded up the steps three at a time and dealt with the door in the same manner. 'Old man! Where are you?' she called.

No one was in the room but from a quick glance she saw that the place was stuffed with treasures. Taking the next flight up, she found a bedroom also furnished with silks, satins and priceless paintings. The bed was empty, sheets rumpled. Up another flight to the very top of the windmill she found a storeroom where the time thief had placed the booty he did not have room to display: chests of gold, jewels and antiquities. Had she failed Mel? Had they not been quick enough to stop the thief slipping away again?

'There's no one here!' she shouted.

Quasimodo, who had shadowed her this far, surprised Eve by leaping out the window and on to the roof.

'Quasi – be careful!'

'Me be fine!' He swung from an old wooden spar that once held the sail, taking a complete view of the roof and surroundings from his bird's eye position. He jumped nimbly back inside, landing like a cat on his feet.

'No one, Eve. Bad old man not here.'

Eve gave him a hug, as much for her own comfort as

to congratulate him on his initiative. She hated it when her little friends put themselves at risk. 'Thank you for looking.'

'You welcome. You, Mel – my friends.'

'Yes, we are your friends.' Eve sniffed. Now was not the time for tears. Even if the time traveller wasn't here, there still might be a clue. She could hear voices below as the policemen greeted the sight of the recovered treasures with glee. 'We'll search up here.'

'Eve, we're looking for any indication as to where – or when – the thief might have taken Mel,' called Cain. 'Information about his identity would help – addresses he has used in the past and future.'

As Quasimodo couldn't read, Eve set him to the task of opening boxes to eliminate those that only held useless valuables rather than documents. She quickly scanned each pile, trying to find anything that would give them a key to the man's identity. It seemed a real hotchpotch of magazines and museum brochures, prospectuses for gentlemen's clubs, opening times for stately homes. Perhaps the twins could make the men downstairs talk? In their forced entry, they had left at least one conscious and the other would probably wake up soon. From the brief glimpse she'd caught of him under the door, he looked a bruiser, the kind who would have been knocked down before. She had no fears for his recovery.

'Big box paper,' said Quasimodo, hefting a suitcase

full of newspapers on to the floor in front of her. Eve flicked through them. On the top lay one folded to an inside page dated from a few decades before. This wasn't like the other material that appeared related to the places he had burgled. What had caught the time thief's interest? He had put a pencil mark around a story of the owner of a rag and bottle shop disappearing in what the reporter put down to a rare case of 'spontaneous combustion'. She wondered if she understood the English phrase correctly. It sounded like that meant he had caught fire without any cause. And the name of the victim was recorded as a Mr Krook.

'This might be something. Thank you, Quasi. We'll take this to the twins.' Brushing off her knees, she went down the creaking stairs. One policeman stood on guard in the room containing the Mona Lisa. His eyes were on stalks as he took in the riches on display.

'They're downstairs interrogating the suspects, miss,' he said. 'Never seen the like, have you? We've found our thief's lair, sure as eggs are eggs. It's a grand result for Scotland Yard.'

'But no Mel Foster.'

'Who? Oh, the boy. Shame but there you are: you win some, you lose some.'

Disgruntled with the policeman's dismissal of Mel's plight, Eve reached the ground floor. Mowgli and the wolves sat in a circle around one thug and the dog that had been under the kitchen table. Sweat beaded on the man's brow. The dog's tail was firmly between its legs. Mowgli said nothing, just stared at the man with his wolfish eyes, more scary even than Grey Wolf's implacable gaze. Abel and the second policeman were trying to revive the bruiser who had been crushed under the door by the application of a jugful of cold water to his face. Cain stood on guard, revolver covering the entrance in case the thugs had other allies not yet known about.

'Find anything?' he asked.

'This.' She held up the paper. 'It says a man named Krook vanished over thirty years ago. At the time the press explained his disappearance as this phenomenon they call spontaneous combustion – have I got that right?'

'Ah yes. A dubious theory that some people have a body chemistry that makes them prone to sudden death in the right electro-static conditions. Highly suspect.'

'He owned something called a rag and bottle shop. What is that?'

'A dealer in second-hand goods. A picture is beginning to form.' With a quick check at the quiet street outside, Cain took the paper from her and scanned the article. 'We think the machine was made in this time period of 1895. The original maker of the time machine sends it back in history, to who knows when? It passes from hand to hand looking to all the world like an unfixable clock until it ends up by chance in the grubby fingers of someone who works out how to make it function. Or maybe he did that first by accident.'

'Yes, brother, that sounds more likely, don't it?' Abel grabbed the groggy man by the back of his collar and gave him a reviving shake. 'Pull a certain combination of levers and, pow! He's gone without a word to anyone, setting fire to the place as the machine rips him out of his time. He probably dropped his lamp in surprise.'

Cain slapped the man's cheeks to add further incentive to his revival, talking to his brother over the man's shoulder. 'People look for him and can only explain his vanishing act as spontaneous combustion. No one thought of time travel back then.'

'I wouldn't think of it now – not unless I'd seen the proof. So, man, what've you got to say for yourself? Do you work for a cove called Krook?'

'Wha–?' The man's head lolled from side to side. Eve wondered if she had underestimated the power of her blow to the door.

'Ask the other one,' she suggested.

Grey Wolf growled. The thug and his dog both flinched.

'I would speak now if I were you, or I will ask my brother wolves to show you what we do to creatures in the jungle who displease us,' said Mowgli in a pleasant tone of voice.

'Yes!' The man's voice was several panicked tones higher than normal. 'The house belongs to Krook. We were here to . . . to keep an eye on him. But he's gone – not come back.'

'What about the boy?' asked Eve.

'What boy? I've seen no boy. Krook went out on a job but he ain't returned, that's all I know.'

Eve feared he was telling the truth. He had none of the signs of someone lying, meeting her eyes straight on.

'Ladies and gentlemen, I think we should take these two down to the station to be questioned further about the thefts,' suggested the policeman. 'I also need to summon back-up to remove the goods. If we leave them untended in this neighbourhood, they'll be gone and sold off the back of a barrow on the Ratcliff Highway before you know it.'

Cain held up a finger. 'In a moment, officer. We've got a friend to rescue first. Why are you here?' he asked the thug. 'The house shows all the signs that it is a single man's private retreat. Did he hire you to look after it in his absence?'

The man dropped his gaze and opened his mouth to reply but Cain forestalled him. 'But no, he could come back any time he wanted – that's rather the point of time travel. In theory, it should barely be left untended. You were here to keep an eye on him, you said. So who sent you?'

'Won't say.' The man folded his arms, looking defiant even though the pack bared their teeth.

'What about you?' Abel shook the man he was holding.

'No, I won't squeal.' The thug wiped a trickle of blood from his lip. 'Believe me, guv, whatever you threaten won't be as bad as what he'd do to me.'

'He?' Cain swooped on the hint. 'Who is "he"? Is it the one they call the Inventor?'

Despite looking doubly shifty, both men refused to budge on this point, even with the pressure of the Jekylls' threats and the intimidating presence of the monsters and wolves in the room. Eve thought that was proof enough: she knew of no other person alive who could inspire such fear.

'It is him, isn't it? He's sent Mel Foster, his own son, back in time, just as we suspected,' she whispered to Cain as the two villains were sent off under police guard, the dog muzzled and led away on a short lead. A cat, released from the outhouse by Mowgli, came back in and wound round Eve's ankles.

'I fear so. We know he wanted to punish his son.'

'So how are we going to save Mel Foster?' She picked up the cat and let it lick her face.

Cain pressed her forearm in comfort. 'Eve, think about it: the only way back is with the time machine. Mel could return more or less the same time as he left, no matter how long it takes him to resolve the obstacles he has met with in the past. If he's not back by now, I am very much afraid that means he will never return.'

Eve shook her head, tears dazzling her gaze. 'I won't accept it. Mel Foster is not lost in the past. He is my friend. He will come back to those who love him. I know it.'

Cain patted her arm then tickled the cat under the chin. 'I hope you are right, Eve.'

Mel was close to panicking. He had been hot on the heels of Krook after all, but had he been just a day too late?

'What do you mean he's gone, Mr Faraday? Gone as in travelled off on the time machine, or gone as in left the room?'

The scientist waved to the door. 'He went that way – stormed out of here, annoyed that my battery was insufficient to work his machine. The rudest man I've met in a long time.'

All was not lost. 'Did he leave an address – please say he was going to come back?'

'I'm afraid we had a bit of a tiff about his manners. He demanded we make him a more powerful source of electricity and I told him with that attitude he could go take a long jump off a short pier. I rather lost my temper, I'm afraid.'

Mel groaned and put his head in his hands.

Mr Faraday patted his shoulder. 'Do you mean to say that his mechanism really works? That it really is a time machine?' He pulled out a journal and opened it to an entry marked for the day before. 'I sketched what I could remember of the interior of the machine but I still can't fathom how it works. Maybe time is more like light in substance and so, theoretically, can be bent by a powerful enough magnetic field? Hmm, that is an intriguing possibility.'

'I've no idea how it works; I just know I broke it.'

'You? With that animal magnetism of yours?' Faraday added a note to his entry. 'How much power do you have in you, young man? If I may make an observation, you don't look as if you'd have very much at all.'

'Looks can be deceiving.'

'So it would seem. When you made that little storm in the bell jar, how much of your power would you say you were employing?'

Mel shrugged. 'A tiny bit. I don't like to let too much out in case I hurt someone. To be honest, I often forget I have it.' He wished he had remembered when Bill Sikes the thug had waylaid him but he had been too busy defending himself with a broom – a broom of all things! He needed something metal if he was going to make himself a weapon to keep violent men at arm's length.

'So you have it under control then? That's very clever of you.'

Mel got up and began to prowl the laboratory. If he was going to be stuck in 1835 for much longer, he needed something to protect himself. 'Not so much clever as instinctive. I usually know very clearly how much energy is required to do something. My friends have tested me and I've lit up a light bulb before without blowing the element.'

'A light bulb? What a fascinating idea. That's beyond us at the moment and we certainly can't make anything as small as your friend's time machine.'

'He's not my friend; call him my enemy rather. And it certainly wasn't his to start with. He didn't make it.'

Faraday put down his pen and folded his hands on the table. 'Forgive me if I strike you as a little slow to believe you but I think I am coming round to considering that you are telling me the truth. The problem is that what you are suggesting is so beyond what I know to be possible in science that my brain is protesting that this must be a hoax. You aren't in league with Krook, are you? You're not here to make me think again about building a bigger battery as he wants?'

'Why would I do that? I seem to be more powerful than anything you've got here so wouldn't it be a waste of your time and mine?'

Faraday clapped his hands together. 'That's it! It's obvious really.'

'What?'

'To make that machine work again, that blackguard Krook needs the world's most powerful source of electricity to replace the one that is broken. You, my dear boy, are the only thing I know that stands a chance of making it do so.'

'But I broke it.'

'You didn't, I presume, know what you were doing at the time?'

'No, I was just trying to make him stop.'

'Then this time, you will want to make it start, won't you? You have control. You just need to apply it to the machine. Oh how I'd love to see that – real time travel before my eyes!'

'So Krook won't be going anywhere without me?'

'Not quickly, that's for certain. There are others who know how to construct batteries. He will be applying to them, I expect. But it won't be a quick project; I know that from experience, even if he does persuade them. That gives us time to find him. Ha-ha! Time to find the time machine!' Faraday made a few more notes, humming under his breath.

While the scientist was engaged in his journal, Mel found a promising looking metal rod on a workbench. 'What's this?'

Faraday glanced up. 'Oh, that old thing? I use it for stirring certain volatile fluids.'

'Can I have it?'

'Of course. But what do you want it for?'

'To channel my energy.'

'Interesting. Well, if you are going to send your power into the machine, you'd better practise controlling the flow. Show me.' Faraday put his pen down and sat back. 'Send your power into that pile of wood by the

190

hearth. It shouldn't harm the logs.'

'Right.' Mel grasped the rod tightly, shoulders tense with the strain of sending the force out of his hand and into another object in a controlled stream. So far he had only used short bursts.

'Ready when you are,' said Faraday.

'Humph.' Mel screwed up his eyes and let go. The power leapt out of the very core of his body, somewhere just below his ribs, rushed down his arm and jumped to the rod. The room cracked and fizzled. Mel could smell burning. Gingerly he opened his eyes. Where once had been a neat stack of logs, now lay a blackened wreck of split timber.

'Fascinating – like a lightning strike.' Faraday picked up the pen and scribbled a description in his book. 'You might want to practise that if you are intending to use it again. Outdoors next time.'

Mel tucked the rod in his back pocket. His neck was aching. 'Yes, you might be right.'

'You probably don't need the rod. You are the conductor – your whole body.'

'But I find it easier to send the power out of me by touching another object, like that rod, or when I zapped Krook, or that boy in the demonstration.'

Faraday rubbed the bridge of his nose thoughtfully. 'Perhaps, but consider lightning. It leaps from the sky to the earth with no bridge between. It is attracted to the target. Maybe it is a question of focusing the attraction so you narrow the field in which your power flows?'

A clock on the wall struck five. Blotting his last entry, Faraday shut up his journal. 'This really is the most interesting day I've had in a long while but I must be going, I'm afraid. Sir Leicester and Lady Dedlock are giving a dinner in my honour and it would be shocking manners to let them down. Do you have somewhere to stay?'

Mel nodded. He'd promised to meet Dodger outside.

'Come back tomorrow. I'll see if I can cast any more light on your Krook's location by asking around at dinner tonight. There will be many of my scientific colleagues in attendance.'

Mel cast a regretful look at the biscuit tin. He doubted his dinner would be as fine.

'Ah, I was forgetting! Your pay.' The scientist reached into his pocket and handed over five shillings, a very generous sum for an hour of standing around having fun.

'Thank you.'

Faraday patted Mel's shoulder. 'Keep your spirits up. We'll find him.'

'But where would he go? I mean, I have to wonder who would I go to if I were him? By the great Isambard, I really must find him – and soon!'

'Isambard?' Faraday laughed. 'You're not talking about that young engineer who almost drowned the other year in the Thames Tunnel? He's got a bit of a reputation for taking wild risks.'

Well, thought Mel, *in my time that wild engineer is one of the most celebrated men of the century, pictured everywhere with his stovepipe hat and cigar.* Cain and Abel had a portrait of him in their laboratory and called him their inspiration and hero. 'It's just a turn of phrase.'

'Isambard Kingdom Brunel – what a name. What were his parents thinking? But it's not a bad suggestion. If he's become a byword in your day, maybe Krook would also think of him. Indeed, if I had a mad request for someone to build something impossibly big and difficult, he is the engineer I would pick.'

Mel felt a glimmer of renewed hope. Maybe it wasn't so impossible to find Krook as the time thief wasn't a very educated man. He would only know of very few experts from this era, just as Mel could only summon up a name or two. They would likely be following a similar trail of breadcrumbs home. 'Where can we find Brunel?'

'Leave it to me. I'll make some enquiries. Come back tomorrow morning.' Faraday put on his jacket and fastened the buttons. 'Oh, and Mel, you can take the biscuits with you.'

Mel shared the sweet spoils of his visit with Dodger who was waiting as he had promised on Albemarle Street.

'Is that all you got? Biscuits?' asked Dodger, who nonetheless seemed happy enough to chomp his way through a handful.

'And some valuable information.'

Dodger nodded sagely. 'Useful commodity that. So can we break into the Institute? A handy little window left open somewhere?'

'That's not what I meant.' Mel's attention was caught by the delicious smells coming from a cook shop. 'Fancy a pie?'

Dodger licked his lips. 'Always. But I wouldn't try that establishment, Doorstop. The woman in there is an old dragon – eyes in the back of her head, and knees, rear end and everywhere monsters can have eyes.'

Mel tightened his fist around his earnings in the depths of his pocket. He was catching on that you couldn't be too careful around Dodger. 'Watch how it's done, my friend.' Sauntering into the steamy warmth of the shop, Dodger trailing doubtfully a few paces behind, Mel went up to the counter. 'Hello.'

The woman gave him an assessing stare, finding him hard to place. A little battered around the edges but smartly dressed in his uniform, he could be a legitimate customer. One thing she was sure about though. 'Oy, you, scat!' she said to Dodger as he examined a basket of rolls.

'He's with me,' Mel said quickly. He put a shilling on the countertop to do the speaking for him. 'Two

194

chicken and gravy pies, please.'

The shop owner was not one to argue with money paid up front. 'Right, young sir. Shall I wrap them?'

'No, we're going to eat them straight away.'

She offered him the whole tray so he could take his pick. 'Wait while I get you your change.'

Balancing two pies in one hand, Mel pocketed the pennies and strolled out of the shop. He tossed one of the pies to Dodger. 'That's how it's done.'

'Cor, you actually bought something?' Dodger took a huge bite. 'My, and they're still hot.'

'Yes, you see you don't have to run a mile with what you stole before eating it. One of the advantages of a law-abiding life.'

'Where did you get the money?'

'The scientist turned out to be a decent man. He paid me for helping him.'

The Dodger's mouth fell open, displaying an unedifying glimpse of half-chewed pastry and chicken. 'What? You got a *job*?'

'Yes, indeed.'

The Dodger swallowed his mouthful. 'I don't think I've ever met anyone, not to talk to, like, that's had one of those. Was it boring?'

Mel thought about electrocuting John Reed and smiled. 'Oh yes, very tedious.'

Dodger nodded as if that settled something. 'Thought so. I'll stick to what I know then.'

Mel had a sudden panic that he had just set the Dodger off on a path the future had not intended him to take. 'It wasn't that bad really. I got to help out in the lecture.'

'All that blah-blah-blah big words palaver? That's not my idea of fun. Let me tell you about what I got up to at the Abbey. You won't believe how easy it is to nick stuff when people are praying.'

Letting Dodger chatter on, Mel finished his pie. On second thoughts, Mel doubted the Dodger had the nature of a boy who in any timeline would welcome a regular job. His instinct was to live dangerously; stealing gave him a rush to the head and a quick way of earning the next crust. He was unlikely to change unless something extraordinary – more extraordinary than a time-travelling boy – crossed his path.

When they arrived at Fagin's lodgings they found him arguing over some goods spread out on the table with a great bear of a man. The stranger had his back to Mel but from the width of his shoulders and the size of his fists, it was clear this wasn't a man to cross. A bull terrier sniffed around his heels, growling menacingly when it spotted the boys enter. Dodger gave Mel a warning nod, indicating they should slide in and make themselves scarce in the back room.

'Come on, you old skinflint, those notes are worth more than ten pounds!'

'But Bill, my dear, you don't know how difficult it is

to pass off banknotes when they've been stolen. They've got numbers – they're like marked men ready to be scooped up by the peelers.' Fagin pawed the paper on the table. 'They may say fifty pounds on the front, but to be turned into cash, I have to go through people that take a cut. They then sell to others who take theirs and so on all the way to France where they can be cashed in on the foreign exchange. Ten is the maximum I can give you without losing money on the deal.'

'I don't believe you.' The man kicked a footstool across the room, narrowly missing Nancy who was sewing red silk flowers on to a battered bonnet. She didn't even flinch. 'Toby Crackit and I take all the risks and you take the cream off the top of the milk. I'm not having it.'

Toby Crackit? Mel had heard that name before on the very night he arrived in 1835. He had a terrible foreboding that he knew who the stranger was.

Fagin noticed the boys enter and took advantage of the distraction. 'Ah, Dodger, a successful day I trust?'

'Not bad, Fagin.' Dodger emptied his pockets of his gains, which included several purses with coins that had been intended for the collection plate.

'And young Master Foster, what did you get up to?' But Mel was speechless. He was face to face with the bruiser who had attacked him, picked his pockets and left him flat on his back in the street for the Dodger to find. The coincidence was too good to be true.

'Fagin!' growled Bill. 'I want fifteen quid or I'll find myself another fence.'

'Eleven,' snapped Fagin.'

'Thirteen – that's my final offer.'

'Done.' Fagin snatched up the banknotes and stuffed them inside his dressing gown. 'I'll get the money for you later. You know my word is good on that.'

'Only because you know I'll skin you if you break it.' Bill went to the hole in the wall and threw his hat and stout walking stick into the room beyond. 'Got any grub?'

As Fagin reluctantly produced some bread and cheese for Bill's supper, Dodger sat down next to Nancy and toyed with the flowers still waiting to be sewn on. He stuck one behind his ear. 'I think Mel's only just twigged to who lives next door, Nance.'

Nancy patted the place on her other side. 'Come and sit down, Mel. Don't mind old Bill.'

'He robbed me,' Mel managed at last to speak.

Nancy shrugged. 'That's what he does, love, and Dodger mops up after him. Didn't you realize?'

'No.' Mel couldn't believe how naïve he'd been. He'd known these people weren't saints but he hadn't connected Dodger to the violent attack on him. Much more serious crimes went on here than stealing a few oranges and handkerchiefs.

'So you did that place last night then, Bill,' said Fagin, handing him a plate. 'I told you the clerks all went home, didn't I?'

'Yes,' said Bill, speaking through mouthfuls, 'but you didn't mention old Marley lived there. We gave him the shock of his life when he found us cracking open his safe at midnight. He looked like he'd seen a ghost.'

'Magic fingers has our Toby when it comes to safes and deposit boxes,' sighed Fagin.

'You broke into Scrooge and Marley's last night?' asked Mel, horror-struck at the idea. This was getting worse by the minute: had he unwittingly brought a set of violent thieves to his friend's door?

'Easiest job I've done in a long while. They're too miserly to have proper guards on the place even with all that cash they have lying around.' Bill patted his bulging pockets, getting a jingling agreement from the coins.

'Did you hurt him?'

'Nah. No need. He couldn't stand up to us, just shook his fist and cursed us. Followed us right out into the street in his nightshirt, would you believe it? He probably caught his death of cold.'

'I hear he's not long for this world,' said Fagin with mock sorrow. 'Got a chill but won't call a doctor as he don't believe in paying for one.'

'I'm with him there. The bloodletters are as likely to kill as cure him.' Bill spread his fingers to the warmth of the fire.

Mel hugged his arms to himself. No, he couldn't be the cause of his friend becoming a ghost, could he? He had never dreamed in even in his darkest nightmares that his travelling back in time was the very reason Mr Marley ended up dead, eventually finding refuge as butler to the Monster Resistance. It was too horrible to contemplate what other disasters Mel was destined to cause in 1835 – and there was a real possibility that he might do something unwittingly to change the future he knew in 1895.

'Old Scrooge is going up and down Cheapside declaring that the burglary is the worst present he ever received and that Christmas is a humbug!' Fagin chuckled. 'He don't seem that worried about his partner, from what I heard. He stands to take over the whole business if Marley kicks the bucket so you might've done Ebenezer Scrooge a favour, Bill.'

Mel wondered frantically if he could go to Marley's bedside and help nurse him. But he would never be allowed in and how could he explain himself in any case? 'I know you in the future as a good ghost' did not seem very persuasive.

'Miserable old coots, the pair of them,' said Nancy, trying on her newly decorated bonnet. 'They deserve everything that's coming to them. Right, Bill, I'm ready. Want to spend a little of your gains on a slap-up dinner at the *Three Cripples*?'

'All right, Nance.' Bill offered his arm in faint imitation of a gentleman escorting a lady. 'Let's go raise a toast to London's two misers who have a little less tonight to be miserly about.'

Mel watched them leave, shocked that Nancy had expressed herself so unfeelingly about someone dying. She was another person he had misjudged. He was well out of his depth. No good would come from him staying here a second longer. He had to find that time machine and get back where he belonged, back to his true friends, to Eve, the mummy, Cain, Abel, Quasi and the monster fairies, none of whom would never rejoice in someone else's misery. Things had got so bad he was even missing Viorica and the wretched wolf pack. He would never complain about sharing his bedroom again.

Chapter Twelve
By the Great Isambard

Since learning that Dodger had been in league with Bill from the beginning, Mel couldn't feel the same way about his friend. Certainly, the Dodger was still amusing and excellent company, but, Mel had to admit, he just couldn't be trusted. Mel would have preferred to have not involved him in the business with Faraday but it was too late for that. Dodger had decided that it was his duty to help Mel so wouldn't hear of being left behind when Mel returned to the Institute the next morning. Mel hoped it was because the Dodger really cared what happened to him, but something told him that his artful friend had multiple agendas.

'You're not going there to do a *job* again, are you?' asked Dodger as if enquiring whether Mel was going to do something abhorrent, like skin live rabbits.

'I've explained already. I have to find that old man who abandoned me.'

'The clock man.'

'Yes. He's got something I need.'

The Dodger's little dark eyes hooked on something across the street. 'I think I need that boy's toffee apple.'

Mel watched with grim resignation as Dodger stole the treat from the unwary child, leaving him in tears as the apple-on-a-stick mysteriously vanished from his hand.

Dodger bobbed up next to Mel as he continued walking along Oxford Street. 'See, easy.'

If the Dodger carried on this path, thought Mel, any spark of the friendly boy he thought he had met would be snuffed out and replaced with a hardened criminal no better than Bill and Fagin. He couldn't resist a comment. 'Congratulations: you've just stolen candy from a baby.'

'Not a baby.' The Dodger took a big bite out of the apple that had been up his sleeve. 'A five year old, maybe.'

'The degree of difficulty is the same. Don't you ever want to do anything better than that, Dodger?'

'You mean rob big houses like Bill?'

'That wasn't what I had in mind. Save lives, stand up for justice?' Like his friends in the Monster Resistance did daily.

'My eyelids, you can talk like a preacher sometimes,

can't you? What's wrong with me the way I am?'

'Ask the child whose toffee apple you've just eaten.'

'His loss, my gain.'

'Exactly.' Mel didn't return the Dodger's wink.

Mr Faraday was waiting for Mel on the steps of the Institute. 'Who's your friend, Mel?'

'Jack Dawkins,' said the Dodger, making a flourishing bow. 'At your service.'

'Charmed, I'm sure,' said Mr Faraday dubiously, patting his watch chain. He had the Dodger's number all right. 'Is he coming with us?'

Mel was about to say no but the Dodger got there first. 'Absolutely. Wouldn't miss this for the world, whatever *this* is.'

'Good thing that I hired a large enough carriage for three.' Faraday signalled to a driver parked further down the street, motioning to him to twitch his pair of horses into a walk. 'Get in, lads.'

'How far are we going?' asked Mel.

'To Swindon.'

'Where?' asked Dodger to whom any town outside London was as mysterious as the Antipodes.

'It's about eighty miles away. It will take us all day so don't expect to be home for supper. Are you still sure you want to come?'

'That's all right, guv, my old man won't worry.' Dodger bounced on the seats until stretching out on the rear-facing one. Fagin wasn't one to fret at the disappearance of one of his boys, unless he thought they might blab to the law.

'Can't we take a train?' asked Mel.

'Not yet.' Faraday winked. 'Give it a few years.'

Mel shut his mouth. He was pleased now that he hadn't said anything to Dodger about time travel. It was too important a secret to trust to him.

'Funny you should mention trains though, Mel, as Mr Brunel is currently surveying the route for the Great Western Railway company. I am reliably informed that we will find him standing in a field somewhere with his theodolite.'

'A theodo-what? This cove in some weird religion?' asked the Dodger, catching the last word.

'Something like that. His religion is Progress,' said Mr Faraday, amused.

The Dodger settled his hat over his eyes to sleep. 'Then my religion is Me First.'

'Why doesn't that surprise me?' muttered Mr Faraday.

Mel spent the journey marvelling at the countryside. He had only been out of London on a ship, never on a jaunt to fields and farms. What he had seen of the country had been from the middle of a river or sailing past out at sea. Close up, he wasn't sure he liked it. Thanks to the recent snowfall, the details of the landscape had been wiped out, leaving the barest outlines of walls, fences, bare trees and tangled bushes.

He had heard that in the spring it was beautiful, bursting with blossom and leaves, but he found that hard to imagine. From what he saw, the country people were as poor as most city dwellers, only with a burring accent, ruddy cheeks and stouter shoes. The coach rattled over the roads, seeming spitefully to find every pothole between each little town. They followed roughly the course of the upper reaches of the Thames, crossing and recrossing it, then over a canal with slow moving barges, before running at a tangent to another loop of the river. Windsor and Maidenhead passed, and then Reading. The river dwindled away to the north as the coach carried on west. As evening fell, they trotted into the little town of Swindon.

'I think we'd best make an early start of it in the morning,' said Mr Faraday, stepping down on to the cobbles of the yard in the middle of the coaching inn. Grooms rushed out of the stable to tend the horses. 'If Brunel is out surveying he will have given up for the night and I've no idea which village he will pick to bed down.' Faraday marched into the inn and got them two rooms on the first floor, one for him, one for the boys. He ordered supper to be sent up to their chamber on a tray, then headed off for his own bed, explaining he had some reading to do.

The Dodger strolled round the little room Mel and he were to share, lifting up all the items of portable property to check their value. 'Do you believe him, about the reading?' he asked, tapping the bottom of a jug then replacing it on the side table with a frown.

'What?' Mel splashed water on his face and rubbed it dry with a linen towel.

'He went off too quick. I reckon he's down in the bar singing songs with the company and flirting with the barmaids.'

Mel thought about this for a moment. 'Mr Faraday? No, I think he's reading.'

'A shilling on him having a knees-up downstairs.'

'You're on.'

The only way to test the bet was to go and look. The boys headed down to the ground floor, slipping between the guests coming and going in the flagstone passageway. Raucous singing came from a room on the left. Dodger peeked round the door into the public bar. 'Told you.'

Mel handed over a shilling.

Mr Faraday was looking a little bleary eyed when they met him for breakfast.

'Nice time *reading* last night?' asked Dodger.

'Oh yes. Very edifying.' Mr Faraday cleared his throat. 'I've, er, discovered where the survey team is today. Uffington.'

'Bless you,' said Dodger.

'I'm not sneezing. It's a place. Famous for its White Horse.'

'I ain't heard of it so it can't be that famous.' Dodger had decided that anything out of London wasn't all that much to write home about. Not enough people with untended pockets for his taste, he had told Mel. He thought it all very provincial and not sufficiently challenging for a young gentleman of his prospects.

'Can we just go there please?' said Mel. Kept awake by the party downstairs, he had lain in bed last night worrying about Eve and his other friends. While he knew logically that they wouldn't be missing him yet, he still felt he had been away too long. Another of those blasted time paradoxes that he kept stumbling over like weevils in a ship's biscuit.

They headed east out of Swindon in the hired coach, travelling for about an hour until the coachman drew up the horses by the side of the road. It was a bleak place in which he had chosen to stop: a line of hills to the south, a low-lying plain bisected with hedges, a few stands of trees.

'There's a party of men over there, sir,' said the coachman, pointing with his long whip. 'About where the innkeeper said they would be.'

Faraday climbed up beside him, making the carriage shift slightly on its springs. 'You're right. Well spotted. I think we've found them. Wrap up, boys, we've got a bit of a trudge ahead.'

Mel wrapped a coach blanket over his shoulders

while the Dodger turned up the collar of his jacket and swathed himself in a long multi-coloured woollen scarf.

'Where did you get that?' Mel asked, not having seen it before.

'A man put it on a back of a chair in the bar last night. I heard him say his granny knitted it for him.' Dodger scrunched up his forehead. 'We're not going back to that inn, are we?'

Looking for a bright side, Mel decided that the granny would probably be happy to knit a second as it looked as though it would be rather fun to put together the rainbow colours. 'No, you're all right. We're heading back to London after this.'

Dodger jumped down into the snow. 'Ugh. There's mud under it.'

'There's mud under it in London.'

'But this mud is made out of the stuff that comes out of cows.'

'In London it's made of the stuff that comes out of horses, dogs and people.'

The Dodger was not to be convinced that London had an equally repellant form of dirt in its own way. 'It's not natural.'

They climbed the stile after Mr Faraday.

'I think you'll find it's very natural. I mean where do you think milk comes from?'

'The dairy. Wouldn't touch it myself.' Giving him a wicked grin, the Dodger jostled Mel as he jumped off the stile. 'They mix it with water and worse round us. Gin is the only safe drink.'

Mel tripped him in return, making them both laugh. 'I prefer tea.'

'Oooh, tea! Listen to the flash cove! Tea served in a silver teapot, I expect?' The Jekylls' teapot was indeed silver. 'China cups and everything lah-di-dah?'

If you thought a mummy pouring it and a giantess offering you sugar while a vampire looked on hungrily was lah-di-dah. Oh steamships, he was even missing Viorica! Things had to have reached critical point for that to happen.

'Excuse me, sirs!' Faraday waved the rolled umbrella he carried. 'Might you be so kind as to tell me where I can find Mr Brunel?'

A man stood up from an instrument that looked something like a camera as it stood on tripod legs. Mel had to remind himself that they didn't yet have photographic equipment.

'I'm Brunel. Isambard Kingdom Brunel. I assume it is me and not my father, Marc Brunel, you seek?'

Mel allowed himself a little moment of hero worship. He was standing in the presence of one of the most remarkable men of his century, one whose name was as venerated as that of the great Darwin, the famous Nightingale, and the revered Stephenson. Brunel did not disappoint, looking uncannily like his statues. A robust man, he wore a black three-piece suit – trousers, jacket and waistcoat – but the legs were splashed with mud up to the knees. He had a black cravat tied in a bow around his rumpled shirt collar and mittens to protect his fingers. A few years younger than Faraday, he made quite a dashing figure with his thick black hair, long sideburns, cigar tucked in the corner of his mouth, and trademark stovepipe hat.

'I want a hat like that,' sighed Dodger.

Mel elbowed him. 'You will not steal Brunel's hat, you hear me? That would be . . . sacrilege.'

The Dodger shrugged. 'It's just a hat.'

'It's not just a hat. It's a whole part of our history summed up in one item of headwear.'

'Mr Brunel, I apologize for disturbing you,' continued Mr Faraday.

'I know you, don't I? Aren't you supposed to be giving a lecture this afternoon? My father has a ticket.'

'Ah well, yes, er, something came up. My colleague is giving my talk for me. I'll be back in time for tomorrow's.'

Brunel waved to a man standing at the far end of the field holding a pole. 'Take a rest, George. How can I help you, Mr Faraday? I'm afraid I can't speak for long as we don't get much daylight at this time of year and I've had far too many interruptions lately.'

'I'm looking for a man called Krook.'

'I see.' Brunel puffed on his cigar.

'He abandoned that child.' Faraday gestured to

where the boys were standing. The Dodger took off his hat and looked sorrowful. 'No, the other one.'

Mel waved.

Brunel narrowed his eyes. 'What's that to do with me?'

'We think he might apply to you to build something for him. You're our only hope of catching up with him. Has he done so?'

Brunel tapped the ash from the end of the cigar into the trodden snow. 'You're the expert on electricity, battery manufacture in particular, aren't you?'

Faraday agreed that he was.

'Why isn't he coming to you?'

'He did but we, er, argued.' Faraday flushed. 'I found him rather rude to tell you the truth.'

'I see. Well, Mr Faraday, I wanted to consult with you in any case. I sent my father to speak to you after your lecture so it's very odd and rather convenient to find you've tracked me down to a field in Uffington.'

'Bless you,' murmured Dodger, grinning at the company.

Brunel ignored him and looked over their heads to the line of hills beyond. 'You know, one day soon you'll be able to travel along the bottom of this valley and admire the White Horse from a steam train window. It's up there under the snow, a relic of an ancient civilization. Some old man probably objected when his tribe chalked it on the Downs, not holding with newfangled nonsense. Those old men still exist. It's people like us, Mr Faraday, who will shake up this century, changing old ways and bringing in better, but does the government understand? No, we have to struggle for every penny.'

'You don't need to tell me. I have to rely on other people's generosity for funding my scientific research.'

Brunel nodded, acknowledging a kindred spirit. 'You found Mr Krook rude; I found him rich. He has promised to give us the money to restart work on the Thames Tunnel, which we are digging Rotherhithe to Wapping. We've not been able to complete the project since the last accident.'

'In which you almost lost your life.'

Brunel shrugged. 'The rewards are worth the risk. This is the first time anyone has attempted to build such a long tunnel under a river. It will revolutionize travel in London. I accept the hazards as all part of an engineer's job.'

'Job!' Dodger spat in the snow. 'Told you they were bad things, Mel.'

'And what did he ask you for in exchange for the money?' said Faraday.

'I'm to build him the biggest battery yet. I propose to construct it down there in the tunnel where we can contain any accidents. I've used the tunnel before for experiments and I think it will be ideal for constructing a potentially dangerous machine.'

Mel stepped forward. 'Mr Brunel, can you tell us where we can find him?'

The engineer shook his head. 'Sorry, no.'

'Oh.'

'But I can tell you where he will be on New Year's Eve.'

'You can?'

'I'm meeting him in the tunnel to survey the site. Eight o'clock in the evening, when I return to town.'

Delivered back to London later that day, Mel and the Dodger trudged across London to their lodgings.

'What is it that the old man's got that you're so desperate to get your hands on, Mel?' asked Dodger for the tenth time.

'I told you, he has something I need to get home.' Mel was congratulating himself on the success of their little trip. Hand finding the metal rod he'd taken from Faraday's laboratory, he turned it over in his pocket, imagining how he would use it. He now had the time and place where Krook would be. The time traveller didn't know it yet but he needed Mel's power to get back to 1895. Krook was going to get one big surprise when Mel turned up to demand a passage home.

The Dodger scratched his head. 'But you live here in London. You said so.'

'In a way.'

'If you've lost your key, you could just knock on the door, or break a window.'

'It isn't that easy.'

'Why isn't it that easy?'

'It just isn't, all right?'

Dodger clearly wasn't happy with his new friend and his evasive answers. Spotting an acquaintance near Seven Dials he ran off, leaving Mel to walk the last mile alone. Mel had never felt lonelier. He was grateful that Dodger and Fagin had taken him in at the beginning of this adventure and made him welcome, but he would never consider himself at home there, not with Bill next door and the evidence of more serious crimes piling up on the table. The games had been fun though, Nancy cheerful, and Dodger could always make him laugh, so it was still as good a place as he could find for the moment. Hopefully it wouldn't be for much longer. Mel could almost taste his desperation to return to 1895, like a bitter flavour in his mouth. The Monster Resistance were a rough pack, a bit like Mowgli's wolves, but there was no question that they were loyal to each other.

'I will find Krook; I will make that machine work; I will get back to my time, or die trying,' vowed Mel.

Eve stood outside what once had been Krook's rag and bottle shop, address recorded in the newspaper article. The Monster Resistance were tracing all the places where they knew Krook had been in the past, speculating for lack of other ideas that he might have dumped Mel there. She would accept finding her friend seventy years older than when she last saw him if that was the only way she could be reunited with him. But hopes of finding Mel as an old man were dashed. The old building had been knocked down and in its place was a smart apartment block for lawyers. Two scuttled past her now, giving her a wide berth and casting anxious looks in her direction. She wondered if her hat was adrift. She had worn her best one, the straw boater with a striped ribbon, because Constable Wilkins had agreed to escort her to Krook's shop. He had offered to demand entry if necessary, but unfortunately his services would not be required.

The constable rejoined her after making enquiries of locals with the longest memory. 'I'm sorry, Miss Eve, but it doesn't looks like Mel was ever here. I asked an elderly chap sitting in Lincoln's Inn Fields and he said the houses were knocked down twenty years ago. He remembers the rumours about Krook blowing up, not something you'd forget in a hurry, I'd say, but hasn't seen him since, and recalls no one of the name of Mel Foster living in the area.'

'Frédérique, what will I do if I don't get Mel Foster back?' Eve felt as if her heart was failing. Maybe the life force that kept her body going was dying along with her hopes for the one who reanimated her?

'Oh, Miss Eve, it won't come to that. He struck me as a resourceful young monster. He'll find his way home.'

Eve shook her head, tears running down the scars on

her cheeks and dripping to the floor.

Wilkins shuffled his feet awkwardly, not sure what to do in the presence of feminine weeping. 'Buck up, miss. My Uncle Ezra had a racing pigeon once, Queenie, he called her, his pride and joy. He took her to Southend and let her go off the end of the pier. She circled up into the air and vanished. He went home expecting her to turn up that night and did she?'

'I don't know.' Eve didn't have much experience of pigeons.

'No. Not a feather for a whole month. Then, one morning, as he was going out to feed his other racers, who came flapping out of the sky, looking a little worse for wear?'

'A bat?' Eve was more used to them than birds, what with Viorica's comings and goings.

Constable Wilkins gave her an odd look. 'No, not a bat. Queenie! He reckoned she'd been to France, decided she didn't like the life, and came home.'

'And you think Mel Foster is in France?'

Wilkins sighed. 'No, I mean I think he's on his way back, just taking his time. Live in hope, Miss Eve. Never give up.' He squeezed her hand then let go quickly.

Eve felt a tingle right down her spine at his touch. 'Oh Frédérique, you are a wonderful friend.'

He blushed scarlet. 'Thank you, miss.'

'It has meant a lot to me that you have accompanied me this afternoon.'

'No trouble at all. Since your lot found all those stolen goods, we've been told at Scotland Yard that full cooperation is the name of the game.'

Eve didn't think that sounded a very good game. She preferred dominoes. 'Then might we walk a little while in the park together? Just the two of us?' She tried batting her eyelids but Wilkins was looking at his watch.

'That would be splendid, but another day. I promised my old mum I'd sort out the coal cellar for her.'

'I could sort out the coal cellar with you, and meet your mother,' Eve suggested tentatively.

'Oh, er, I'm afraid that's not a good idea. She's not a woman with liberal ideas, my mum. Doesn't like monsters.'

Eve didn't think of herself as a monster. She knew the others enjoyed the label but she preferred to consider herself just a largish young lady. 'That's all right then, as I'm not really a monster.'

'Hah-hah-hah!' Wilkins cut off his laugh when he saw that she wasn't joking. 'Oh, but you are to me, a wonderful monster! And so is the mummy, a splendid chap – and Mr and Mr Jekyll, astonishing. And did you see how ugly the monster fairies looked in their new dresses? Quite the best entertainment I've seen since *The Pirates of Penzance*, I can tell you.'

'Is that what we are to you – marvels and amusements?'

'No! You're brave and interesting, noble and true. Different, yes, but different in all the good ways people can be different.'

Eve felt the mist lift from her eyes. Just before he had been whisked away, Mel had tried to warn her, hadn't he? If only she had listened and not been caught up in fussing over foolish hats, he might still be with her – she might have moved fast enough to stop him being taken. 'But when you look at me, you first see my difference from you?'

'Well of course! Why wouldn't I? You're at least seven foot – it's rather hard to miss. And that stitched together thing is quite brilliant. Your maker was a man of genius.'

Anger fizzed inside Eve. 'By your estimation, he wasn't a man but a monster. My father was just like me.'

Wilkins was oblivious to the offence he was provoking. 'Then he was a tip-top monster, clever with his hands. Now, Miss Eve, if we've finished here, I'll walk you back home and then go on to Mum's.'

'It's all right, constable, us monsters don't need an escort.'

'I'm sorry, have I upset you?'

'Go see your mother. Thank you for your assistance this afternoon. Goodbye.' Eve stalked off, knowing he would struggle to keep up with her long strides. Glancing behind she saw that he hadn't followed her but stood on the pavement scratching his head, wondering where he had gone wrong.

'Silly man!' fumed Eve. 'Foolish, hateful me. Why did I think anyone normal could love me?' She had steadfastly refused to see herself as others saw her but now she had to admit she was a little big, and a little patched-together. Would no one see past this? Mel had but he was gone. She was so angry with herself that she did not notice that she was leaving cracked pavers in her wake as she stomped back to Bloomsbury.

Chapter Thirteen

Going Underground

New Year's Eve saw the snow converted to slush under a heavy fall of rain. Mel went to Scrooge and Marley's praying he could be of service but discovered that Jacob had indeed passed away. The office was closed up, a black ribbon tied to the lion-shaped knocker. Standing with the rain dripping down his face in icy tears, he felt as low as he had ever done in his life. If he'd killed Jacob Marley, he might end up exposing the Jekyll twins' secret to their enemies, or cause Eve to be locked up in a zoo – it was impossible to predict the end of the ripple effect of his presence out of time.

221

He had to get back to his own time before he caused any more disasters.

And if he couldn't, what then?

Mel splashed along the pavements, water trickling down his neck, seeping through his shoes and soaking his trouser bottoms. He would have to take himself to a place where he would do minimal damage to the timeline. A desert island perhaps? He could sign on as a cabin boy again and jump ship when he reached a suitable spot. But that would be a miserable existence; he could hardly bear thinking about it. The only thing that would make it worth doing was knowing that his sacrifice saved others in the future and he wasn't even sure that was how the time paradox worked. If he was forced to do it on the rocky basis of 'just in case', then he had to find a way of leaving a message for his friends to tell them what happened.

He would have to think of a method of sending a letter to be delivered in sixty years' time. They might even come and fetch him if he was still alive. No, that wasn't fair on them. What if they found out something bad had happened to him? Better they imagined him happy with his lot. Perhaps Mr Faraday would look after the message and make sure his descendants sent it in the penny post at the right time. He could date it a few days after his disappearance to give them a chance to get used to his absence and give him an opportunity to intercept it if by a miracle he returned first.

'What's up, my covey?' Dodger slid along the top of a low wall down a flight of steps and landed in front of Mel. 'Why the long face?'

'I'm just considering my future.'

'Don't worry: it might never happen.'

'That's what worries me.'

'You're an odd fish, Mel, I have to tell you.'

'A fish out of water, that's for sure.'

'So are you going to meet this cove at the tunnel tonight?'

'Yes.'

'Can I come? You need someone to watch your back.'

'I rather you didn't. In fact, please don't.'

'Righto. If you really don't need me.' The Dodger's agreement was too swift.

'I mean it.'

'I hear you, pal. Want to go see old Marley's funeral?'

'It's today?'

'They're expecting quite a crowd, marking the departure of the late unlamented miser.'

That sounded grim. At least Mel could be there to pay his respects, a genuine mourner. 'All right, but promise you won't pick their pockets?'

'What? At a funeral? I do have some standards!' The Dodger clutched his hat to his chest and raised pious eyes to the heavens.

Mel stood in the freezing rain a few headstones

223

away while Dodger made himself busy in the crowd. He watched the small party of those closest to Marley gather around the freshly dug hole in the city graveyard. The place was packed like a tin of sardines with previous burials but Marley had invested in a family vault so at least other coffins hadn't been taken out to make way.

'We brought nothing into the world, and take nothing out,' began the minister, his black vestments flapping in the chill breeze. An altar boy held an umbrella over his head to protect his prayer book.

The other mourners numbered exactly two: Scrooge and Bob Cratchit, the clerk from the office. Scrooge was mumbling to himself and counting on his fingers; Bob Cratchit shivered in his inadequate coat and looked glum. Around the railings of the churchyard a crowd had gathered. They whispered together and giggled, their earlier shouted insults quieted by the presence of the vicar. It was so incredibly sad.

But Jacob has a good afterlife, Mel reminded himself. He would find a place in a house where he would be loved and respected. Mel made a vow that if he got back to his own time, he would never walk right through Jacob Marley again.

Saying what he hoped was his final farewell to Dodger, Nancy and Fagin, Mel left the lodgings as evening drew on. He looked up once at the lit window, watching Fagin flit across with the frying pan, juggling a string of sausages. For all their flaws, he would miss the thieves if he were successful tonight. Nancy and Dodger had good hearts, even if they lived through bad means. He hoped they'd be all right in the future.

It was fully dark when he met Mr Faraday as arranged on Tower Hill. For some reason he couldn't quite understand, Mel had picked the very same spot to which he had time travelled. Perhaps because it made him feel a little closer to Eve. It was here he had last seen his friend. The scientist arrived in a hansom cab. From the terse exchange of words, it appeared he was having difficulty persuading the driver to stop in this dubious part of town.

'In you get, quick now!' called Faraday, holding out a hand.

Mel jumped inside and wrapped his legs in a blanket to drive away the chill that had stayed with him all day. The springs lurched as if someone might possibly have clung on to the back but, looking out the little rear window, Mel couldn't see anything. He had his suspicions, though.

'How do you want to proceed, Mel, when we catch up with this Krook of yours?' asked Mr Faraday, offering him a ham sandwich from a little hamper. He clearly understood about boys and hunger.

'If you could explain about my power, I think he'd listen to you. You're the expert after all. I just want him to understand that he needs me as much as I need him.'

'I'll try, but what if he doesn't cooperate? He has his

hopes set on his own solution and Brunel might just be able to do it. He can produce wonders, that man.'

'Then I'll think of something else.' The 'something else' involved theft of the time machine, which Krook deserved as he had started this off with a kidnap, but Mel wasn't going to raise that with the law-abiding scientist.

Faraday passed him an apple and polished one for himself on his sleeve. 'There's always a place for you in my laboratory, you know that, don't you?'

'Thank you. That's very decent of you.' But Mel feared he couldn't take it up for all the reasons he had thought through, not without changing history in unintended ways. Being the death of a friend was lesson enough.

The journey to the tunnel entrance on the Rotherhithe side of the river took half an hour even though it wasn't far as the crow flies. At this point in the city's history, they had to double back and cross at London Bridge.

'It would be very useful to have a bridge at the east end of the city,' mused Faraday.

Mel thought of the splendid Tower Bridge that had just been opened in his day. 'It might come, you never know.'

Faraday grinned. 'Ah, but you do, and you're not going to tell me, are you?'

Mel returned the smile. 'Nope. My lips are sealed.'

Faraday shook his head at himself in wonder. 'You know, I really don't think I have got my brain around the extraordinary fact that I'm sitting next to a boy from the future. There must be all sorts of tests I should be running but instead I find myself helping you to escape my investigations.'

'Believe me, it's for the best, sir.'

The hansom cab drew up at the entrance to the Thames Tunnel. It looked to Mel like the entrance of one of the grander Underground stations, something yet to be invented in this period. They entered through a brick archway into an echoing chamber. The constructors had allowed sightseers to inspect the works from the early days of the project so there was a decent ticket hall and an iron staircase winding down able to accommodate large numbers of people. The gates were open and the gas lamps lit, indicating that Brunel was expecting guests.

Faraday checked his pocket watch. 'Ten past. That took a little longer than I anticipated. If Krook was on time he should already be down there with Mr Brunel. Shall we join them?'

Mel felt sick, like a gambler staking his inheritance on the roll of the dice. 'Yes, but can I give you something first?' He handed over the letter he had written. 'This is to my friends in the future. I'm not sure what's going to happen down there, or even if the machine will work properly with me powering it, but would you make sure this is sent on the date I've put on the outside by your descendants?'

Faraday nodded and put the envelope in his breast pocket. 'I'll give it to my solicitors with my will and ask my executors to ensure it is sent at the right time. But maybe you won't need it, Mel.'

'I know – and if I don't, I'll happily tear it up when the postman delivers it in 1895.'

'You're a brave lad. I wish you all the best and every happiness *whenever* you end up.'

Despite the lighting, the steps down were spooky. They fixed to the wall like spirals on a conch shell, open fretwork of fancy wrought iron that clanged as heels struck it. The shaft was much bigger than Mel expected, the far side lost in shadows as they wound their way down. The workings had been closed up after the last catastrophic flooding incident in which workers had lost their lives. Brunel survived because he had got to the exit, only to find it had been locked to stop intruders. He was alive today because someone had heard his shouts before the water reached him.

Don't think about that now, Mel told himself.

As they got nearer to the bottom, they could hear voices rising up to them.

'These bays will make an excellent platform for the battery.' Mr Brunel was holding up a lantern to illuminate a sturdy brick structure at the mouth of the tunnel. The entrance was an elegant arch, tall enough to accommodate a driver sitting on top of a horse-drawn coach. 'We are building two parallel tunnels down here and these supporting columns stand between them holding up the roof. At the far end, well beyond the light of my lamp, is the shield, or the tunnelling machine, but that shouldn't interfere with the construction of your device.'

A man moved out the shadows to stand beside Brunel. It was Krook! At last, thought Mel, he had caught up with the slippery time thief.

'How long do you think it would take you, sir?' asked Krook, clutching a maroon valise in his right hand.

'He'll have the time machine in there,' whispered Faraday. 'At least, that's where he kept it when he showed me.'

Brunel lit a cigar and puffed thoughtfully. 'I'm thinking that it's not so much a question of how long but how much? Are you sure you have enough money to cover both the materials for the battery and the restarting of work on the tunnel? I don't mean to question your *bona fides*, Mr Krook, but I don't know you from Adam, do I?'

'I promised you ten thousand pounds, didn't I? Well, this should cover a down payment, to show I'm serious.' Krook pulled a gold bar out of his pocket and slapped it in Brunel's hand. 'I'll give you the rest on completion of the job.'

'He won't,' whispered Mel. 'He'll be long gone. I bet he's planning to double-cross Brunel.'

Brunel dropped the gold bar in the bag he had slung over his shoulder. 'Gold, eh? That'll do nicely, thank you, sir. In that case, I think we can start next month.'

'Next month!' Krook looked close to exploding with frustration.

'The materials have to be ordered, you understand. I don't have the items you specify just lying around at home.'

'Alternatively,' said Mr Faraday, stepping off the bottom tread and approaching the pair, 'you could leave out the building of the battery to power your time machine and use what's on hand, so to speak.'

'What!' squawked Krook, hugging the case to his chest. 'How do you know –? That's nonsense. There's no such thing as a time machine.'

Brunel shook his head, doubtless wondering why a previously sane scientist had come all this way to spout such rubbish. He took a puff of his cigar and blew the smoke straight up like vapour escaping a steam engine funnel.

'Hello, Mr Krook. Remember me?' asked Mel, stepping out from behind Faraday.

'You will notice, Mr Krook, that I'm returning something to you that you dropped on Tower Hill. I've had a most interesting conversation with Mel Foster. It appears that you are in the business of kidnapping.'

'I've done nothing wrong. He's a monster.' Krook jabbed a finger in Mel's direction.

'Steady on,' said Brunel, tapping the ash from the end of his cigar.

'I'm glad you said that,' said Faraday. 'Do you know exactly what kind of monster he is?'

'I don't know and I don't care. Look, I'm having a private meeting here with Mr Brunel. No one invited you along.'

Brunel folded his arms, ankles crossed, shoulders propped against a brick pillar. He looked entertained by this unlikely discussion. 'Actually, I invited them. You want a battery built, correct? Well, I'm only an engineer. You are going to need the world expert as a consultant if you've any hope of making this work.' He gestured with the cigar towards Faraday.

'All right then, I'll pay him too. Consult all you like.' Krook's eyes shone with a mad glint of desperation.

'I accept,' said Mr Faraday quickly. 'And my expert opinion is that you don't need to waste my time or that of Mr Brunel. You've got what you need standing right here in front of you.' He put his hands on Mel's shoulders.

'Where?' Krook looked around at everything but Mel, peering into the damp corners of the tunnel. Mel would have laughed if he hadn't felt so anguished that he might never get home. He had to persuade this horrible man to cooperate. 'What is it?'

'It's not a "what" or an "it". It's a boy. Mel Foster, the only known human source of electricity.'

231

Mel held Krook's gaze as it finally came to rest on him. 'You see, Mr Krook, I am a proper monster, just one you underestimated.'

Krook gaped.

'You want proof?' asked Faraday. 'He broke your machine, did he not? Well, now we've mended the circuit, I'm of the opinion that he is the only one who can make it work – at least until battery technology moves on a few decades. Can you afford to wait that long?'

'And I'll help you this minute if you promise to take me with you back to 1895,' added Mel.

'Mr Faraday, is this all make-believe?' asked Brunel, deciding he'd stood back long enough.

'Call it that if it helps you get your mind round it, Mr Brunel. It is certainly far-fetched, I grant you, involving time machines and boys with powers they really oughtn't to have. So, Mr Krook, are you going to take the solution that I've brought with me, subject to the terms and conditions Mel has for you, or are you going to throw your money away on building something that might not work after all?'

'Here now,' muttered Brunel. 'I could do with that money.'

'Face facts, man: he was never going to pay you the full amount.'

Brunel threw his cigar away. 'I knew it was too good to be true.'

Krook chewed his lower lip, making his resemblance to a rabbit quite striking. 'You think the boy really is the answer?'

'I do,' said Faraday.

'I didn't want to harm you, boy. I was made to – they have my cat!'

'I've friends that can help save your cat,' Mel assured him. 'Who has him?'

'It's a her. Lady Jane. But there's this man – he calls himself the Inventor – he threatened her, with this horrible stick of his. He broke my lovely things then said it was her next if I didn't do what he said. Then he sent round his thugs and their dog to keep us prisoner. I had no choice!'

There was always a choice in Mel's opinion. 'Did the Inventor know it was me you were taking hostage?'

'Of course. It was his idea. He wanted you well out of the way.'

Mel had been expecting something like that but to have his father's cruelty confirmed still came as a blow. 'I promise that I won't hold it against you if you'll just get us back to the same time as when we left. I don't want my friends worrying about me. We'll help you against that man.' *My father*, Mel added silently. *Why did he hate me so much?*

'So what's it to be, Mr Krook?' asked Faraday.

'I suppose there's no harm letting him try, is there?' Krook stroked the maroon leather case, torn as to the

233

best course to take. 'We can still try the battery if you're wrong about him.'

'That's true.' Faraday squeezed Mel's shoulders, warning him not to make a sound in case that sent the finely balanced judgement swinging the other way.

'Then . . . then I agree. I'll set the clock for a few minutes after we left.' Krook went to open the bag, then stopped. 'One thing though, do you know if this tunnel exists in 1895?'

Mel looked for clues in the structures around him but nothing came to mind. 'I'm not sure. I've not heard of it and you'd think I would know if people were able to walk under the Thames.'

'Then we should go somewhere safer. The green by the White Tower is a good place. Nothing has been built on there for centuries.'

A shout came from higher up the staircase. 'Quick! There they are! He's about to do the hand off of the goods!'

Brunel held up his lamp, seeing shadows leaping down the wall. The slanting angle of the gaslight made them look like an army of giants. 'What's the meaning of this? These are private excavations. You can't just barge in here!'

From the din echoing in the space, it sounded like hundreds of feet were thundering down the iron steps. Mel looked up to see Dodger leading Bill and his two partners in crime round the spiralling staircase to the tunnel level. The Dodger! Mel felt the betrayal like a kick in the stomach. Had the Dodger been planning this all along? Had his help always been about the golden clock and never about friendship? Then a pistol shot rang out and Brunel's lantern glass exploded.

'Take cover!' called Faraday, pulling Mel behind one of the pillars inside the tunnel itself. Krook dashed to the one opposite and stood with his back pressed to the bricks. Brunel had opted to stand his ground on the pavement at the bottom of the stairs and, from the sound of fist on flesh, had got into a fight.

'Dash it all! Three against one isn't cricket! I'll have to help him.' Faraday bolted out from behind the column.

Mel wasn't going to hide while his friends got beaten up by superior numbers. Pulling his rod from his back pocket, he came out of hiding. There was a heap of bodies, elbows sawing up and down as wild punches flew, boots and heads rolling in an ungentlemanly scrum. It was hard to tell the men apart, except for Bill that was, who stood on the bottom stair calmly reloading his gun.

Mel knew exactly what to do about that. Calling on his power, he let it flow from his chest, down his arm, into the rod and out to the staircase. It flickered and crackled across the gap like horizontal blue lightning. Accuracy didn't matter as the whole flight of steps became electrified. Bill went rigid, juddering on the spot, hair up on end. The gun fell from his fingers. Alarmed at the amount of power that had sprung from him and that he might actually kill the man, Mel ended the electric current. Bill fell flat on his back, stiff as a board, eyes wide, breathing harsh. Mel hurried over to scoop up the pistol.

But someone else got there first.

'Dodger, don't!' said Mel as his former friend slid out of view behind one of the many pillars down the tunnel, on the hunt for Krook and the golden time machine. 'Please: I thought we were friends!'

His answer was silence. He had to face up to the fact that there was no friendship among thieves.

'Why didn't they make the clock casing out of wood rather than gold?' muttered Mel. It would be impossible to track the Dodger in these shadows but Mel did at least know where Krook was hiding.

'Mr Krook, there's someone with a gun coming to get you,' said Mel, running to where the old man crouched behind a pile of bricks. 'Come on, we've got to hide in a better place than this. We've got to go further in.'

Krook looked frantically back to the staircase, the only way out, and then to the shadows that hid the person after the device. The old man's thoughts were plainly written on his face. If Krook ran with it, he'd be chased; if he passed it over to someone else to look after, he stood a good chance of getting free. 'You can't let them get the time machine, boy!' he said, thrusting the valise into Mel's arms. 'Take it. Keep it safe. I trust you to come and get me. I'll wait for you at the Athenaeum Club.'

'What? But I need you to work it!'

Krook wrung his hands, moaning to himself. 'Oh, Lady Jane, I'm sorry. I know you need me, but I need to stay alive more! I've got to go!'

Taking advantage of the fact that Bill was prostrate at the bottom of the steps and the two other men were engaged in a battle with Faraday and Brunel, Krook darted to the stairs and hared up them. It was just like Tower Hill all over again, except that this time Mel had been left with the encumbrance of the time machine.

All right, I'll hide until I can spot the Dodger, zap him and take him out of the fight, Mel told himself. He ran further into the tunnel, leaving the brightly lit area for the semi-darkness. Brunel had mentioned something called a shield down here. That sounded good: somewhere defendable.

'Oy, Doorstop, hold up. We can split the goods!' called Dodger from his lookout spot in the shadows. The echoes were strange. Mel couldn't get a fix on his location. Was the Dodger trailing or was he already somewhere up ahead?

The last thing Mel wanted was for the time machine to be taken apart. 'No chance, Dodger. You don't know what you're really dealing with here.'

'Nor do you. I've got a gun and I'm sorry, pal, but

there's no honour among thieves. You won't leave here alive if you don't hand it over.'

Valise held close to his chest so it wouldn't bang on any obstacles, Mel crept from bay to bay, trying not to make a sound to give away his position.

The Dodger gave a put-upon sigh. It sounded as if he was level with Mel but he wasn't visible.

A thought struck Mel. Was Dodger using the parallel tunnel?

'Why you being so unreasonable, Doorstop? I help you out of the kindness of my poor old heart and this is how you repay me?'

Now Mel finally understood Dodger's real game from the beginning, it was tempting to point out bitterly that his interests had never featured in the Dodger's priorities, that the Dodger had always been helping himself, but to do so would also give away Mel's position. He was angry but he wasn't going to lose his temper now with his fake friend and lose his advantage.

Backing away, Mel collided with a wooden beam. He guessed he had found the shield. He began climbing, tricky to do while hefting a valise and trying to be silent.

'From what you told us, that clock you're carrying is broken,' said Dodger. 'Give it here and we can split the proceeds. You could become one of us proper like, one of the gang. See, Mel, if you don't hand it over, I'm going to have to take it. It's not worth your life, surely?'

Yes, it was, and now Mel saw that the Dodger was

definitely in the next tunnel. Mel caught a glimpse of him through the communicating bay, creeping along the wall, pistol raised ready to fire. The jolly friend who played with handkerchiefs had swelled into a jungle predator stalking his prey. Even his shadow stretched tall and menacing in the fluttering light of the gas lamps, his tilted hat like a second monstrous head.

'I'm going to find you, you know. They ain't finished the tunnel so there's no way out down here. You won't get past me. I just have to keep on looking. Give up now and maybe I won't shoot you.'

Mel wondered if he could zap Dodger from this distance. He gripped his rod, remembering the scorched pile of logs. The staircase had been easier as there was a huge target to hit and he hadn't had to use much power. To ensure he knocked out Dodger before he got off a shot, Mel would have to let out a full blast – and that might kill the other boy. Mel knew he would hate himself if he took a life and, even without that consideration, there was the question of changing history. Someone might miss meeting the Artful Dodger in the future.

'Darwin's tortoise, what should I do?' muttered Mel.

He looked at the valise that he had placed softly beside him on the top row of the wooden scaffold. For a few moments he would be hidden up here as the Dodger examined all the other compartments used by the excavators in the shield structure. It had been made in sections to protect the workers from rock falls and that fact bought Mel a little more time. This whole thing had been about time, hadn't it? And the Dodger was wrong: there was another way out.

The clasp opened to his touch. Inside lay the time machine, glowing in the faint light of the gaslights. Mel hadn't been close to it since the brief look on Tower Hill in the moonlight and he was amazed at its beauty. The case was smooth and elegant, not out of place on any well-to-do person's mantelpiece, but inside the marvels began. It reminded him of jewellery rather than machinery in its waterfall of tiny cogs and levers. He could see that each was engraved with Roman numerals, tiny scratches guiding the complex calculations needed to manipulate time. More intricate than the Fabergé egg, more powerful than the biggest steam engine: how did it work? If he made a mistake he could catapult himself back to a time where this tunnel didn't exist, entombing himself in river clay and gravel. If he went too far forward, would it be here at all? Or flooded?

Mel could feel a flutter of panic in his chest, like a moth knowing it was circling too close to a flame but unable to stop itself. *Get a hold of your imagination*, he ordered himself. *There is another way out: Krook worked out how to use it and he isn't anyone's idea of a genius. You can hope to do at least as well as him if you try.*

'Come out, come out, Doorstop!' called Dodger, shaking the scaffold as he began climbing.

Mel nudged the hands on the dial to midnight. It somehow seemed appropriate. If he stayed here any longer, he would either be shot or have to kill another boy – neither was acceptable. If he took the risk, he might just get away scot-free. He could then come back and collect Krook from his club as promised. Everyone would be safe.

Another thought nudged into his brain. He, Mel Foster, would be the master of the time machine. With his power to keep it running, he could go anywhere and do anything. He would have something even Cain and Abel could not match; he'd be more powerful than any in the Monster Resistance, the leader rather than the messenger boy who had to beg a place for himself.

The top of a hat appeared level with the platform, then a pale face with its tiger grin. 'Ah, there you are, my covey. Sorry about this, Doorstop, but you're in my way.'

Mel heard the click of a pistol being cocked. 'Not for much longer.' Mel grabbed hold of a tiny gold lever.

The pistol fired.

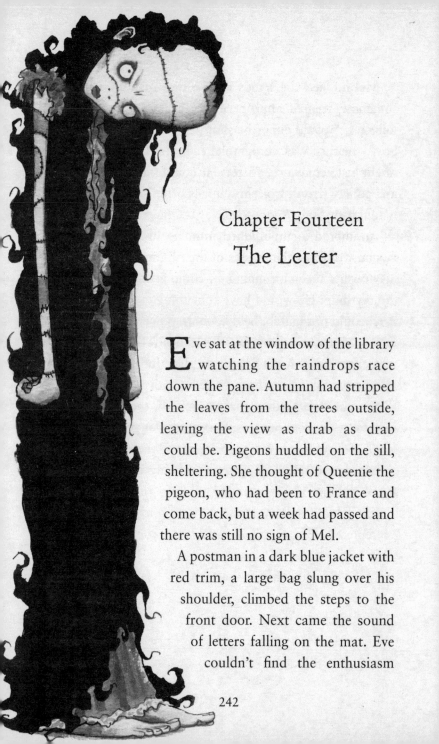

Chapter Fourteen
The Letter

Eve sat at the window of the library watching the raindrops race down the pane. Autumn had stripped the leaves from the trees outside, leaving the view as drab as drab could be. Pigeons huddled on the sill, sheltering. She thought of Queenie the pigeon, who had been to France and come back, but a week had passed and there was still no sign of Mel.

A postman in a dark blue jacket with red trim, a large bag slung over his shoulder, climbed the steps to the front door. Next came the sound of letters falling on the mat. Eve couldn't find the enthusiasm to go and look. All appeals for information about an elderly person called Melchizedek Foster living somewhere in the country had come back negative. The twins were now working on the assumption that Mel had changed his name or gone abroad, which made the search even more hopeless.

'Madam?' It was Jacob Marley bobbing at her elbow. He attempted a smile, which told her how miserable she must look if even the doom-loving ghost felt moved to cheer her up.

'*Oui*, Monsieur Marley?'

'There's a letter for you.' Not able to hold a corporeal object in his disembodied state, he made the envelope levitate across the room with the artful application of ghostly breezes.

'For me?' Eve plucked it out of the air. A few days ago she might have anticipated a love letter from the constable but now she knew better. Wilkins had not come round so often lately and kept his visits mainly to the kitchen where he and the mummy could discuss motorcars. An awkward silence had fallen every time Eve entered. Her romance had hit the rocks before it had even started.

What did any of that matter with Mel Foster still missing? She forced herself to concentrate on the letter. The writing on the front was unfamiliar, a sloping italic hand used by those in the legal profession, but it was clearly her name and the correct address. Marley discreetly drifted away and Eve broke the seal. Her heart did a double thump. Two notes fell out and one was Mel's handwriting. She took that up first.

My dearest Eve,

If you are reading this letter, it means that my attempts to return to you have failed. Perhaps you know by now that the time machine belonged to a man called Krook. While he was carrying me off, I blasted him with my power and we ended up where neither of us wanted – in 1835. I broke the machine, Eve. It was my fault. You must not blame yourself as I know you will try to do. You always think you should stop any harm coming to me but sometimes in life there is nothing you can do to stop bad things happening.

I hope we can mend the machine and I can get back to you, but that is a bit of a long shot if the truth be told. You are not to worry – promise me that. I've made friends here and I will be very happy, apart from the fact that I can't be with you and the rest of the Monster Resistance. Please tell them I send my love, even Viorica – that will annoy her no end. Inky and Nightie can have my stuff and tell them they are top chaps. Look after Quasi. Time travel is a horrible thing and he will need someone to make him feel at home. Say to the mummy that he is the best cook ever and I'll miss him. Give Cain my fondest greetings – I think of him as a true brother in whatever shape he is today. Tell Abel I'll keep up my studies even without him to badger me and ask him to give Viorica a kiss from me. She will definitely prefer that he be the messenger than that I give it in person. And finally, I send you a hug all for yourself. You are the best thing that ever happened to me and I'll miss you so much. If you weren't already on track to meet me sixty years later, I'd be tempted to go and find you now in the Arctic, but what's done is done. I can't play around with the timeline so I'll live quietly somewhere for the rest of my days.

Your friend now and in the past and always,
Mel Foster

Eve was howling by the time she had finished the letter. This was the news she had been dreading. Her shoulders shook in great wrenching sobs that threatened to burst some of her stitches. The noise attracted Cain into the room. Abel stood at the door, took one look at the letter in her hand, then looked away, his eyes suspiciously damp.

'I'll leave you to comfort her,' he told his brother.

Cain nodded. He sat next to Eve on the window seat and held her hand in his strong fingers, giving it a squeeze. 'So we've lost him then? May I see?'

Eve passed him the letter and blew her nose on her handkerchief.

Cain read it quickly, then scooped up the envelope and the other note that had fallen on the floor. 'What does this one say?'

'I haven't read it yet.'

'May I?'

She nodded.

Cain unfolded it and read the contents aloud.

'*Dear friends of Mel Foster. I am writing this to be included with Mel's note as I'm sure you would like news of his last days among us.*'

'Last days?' Eve sniffed. 'What does that mean?'

Cain continued to read.

'*Mel thought he would either get back to his time or be left with me in 1835. I hope he did manage to get home but, in case there is another outcome we did not foresee, I am including this letter along with his note to you.*

'*For the record, I, Michael Faraday, last saw Mel Foster on New Year's Eve 1835.* Michael Faraday! Newton's wig, Mel chose his helpers well! He's a hero of mine,' said Cain. '*He took the time machine with him along the Thames Tunnel as he was being pursued by an armed thief. What happened next is unclear. We heard a pistol shot and then saw the thief, one called Jack Dawkins, running for his life. He shouted that "the doorstop had vanished – time to split, my coveys"*

246

but I'm unclear as to what that meant, not being fluent in thieves' cant. He and his fellow villains ran off before I could have them arrested. I applied to the original time traveller, one Mr Krook, but he was unable to enlighten me. If Mel had gone, he could be in any time. Krook also told me that, now he no longer had the time machine, he had decided he would live out his days at the Athenaeum Club. He asked only that his cat, Lady Jane, an innocent victim in all this, be rescued from her captors and be taken care of in 1895 and I promised to pass on this request to well-meaning people in the future. The address of where she is being held hostage follows.'

Eve wiped her eyes on the curtain as her handkerchief was soaked through. 'I have already rescued her. She is now with the landlady of the *Six Jolly Fellowship-Porters*.'

Cain nodded. '*I have concluded that Mel used the time machine to escape from the one pursuing him but I must tell you that he had no training and would be flying it blind. I hope to God that he chose his moment to emerge correctly. We were in a tunnel under the Thames. Need I say more? I have had nightmares ever since. Please help him if you can.*'

Cain passed the note from Faraday to Eve. 'The Thames Tunnel – we must go there and as quickly as possible.'

Eve's hopes rekindled. 'You mean he might be trapped

247

down in the tunnel, we might be able to reach him?'

'I wish it were that simple, Eve. That tunnel, well it's not how he left it, that's for sure.'

The now expected sensation of an icy storm whipped around Mel. He clutched the time machine, feeding it a steady stream of his power, watching a red hand creep clockwise round the dial until it met the midnight position of the black hands. The glass bulb inside shone with a steady white beam of light, a lighthouse in his darkness. As long as that stayed lit, he knew he wasn't feeding it too much power to blow the circuit again. He mustn't overshoot. The hand counted down to the last five seconds, four, three, two, one.

Mel cut off his power . . .

And found himself in free-fall. He tumbled from what once had been the top of the scaffold to the bottom of the tunnel; the machine flew from his hands and landed with a crack at the same time as he dropped on something metal.

'That hurt.' He moaned, rubbing the back of his aching head. It was completely dark. Mel lay staring up at nothing as he gathered his wits. He didn't think anything was broken, not by way of bones, but he had a horrid feeling the time machine hadn't fared so well. What he could do with was a light to find the device but the bulb had gone out as soon as he withdrew his power.

Odd. The smell of the tunnel had changed too.

Whereas before it had smelt of water seepage, now it had sooty odour.

Something scuttled away from him. A rat?

'When am I?' he wondered aloud. His voice echoed in the tunnel. 'Hello? Is there anyone here?'

No one appeared to be coming to help him. Perhaps he had stopped in a time when the tunnel was closed? Mr Brunel had mentioned he hoped to finish it so that horse-drawn carriages could be driven under the Thames. Maybe those didn't go at night?

Mel sat up and groped the ground around him, seeking the time machine. His hands found a cold metal object, a wooden crosspiece and then another cold metal object like the first. He couldn't move them so they weren't part of his device. He tried to draw up a picture in his mind. He wished he had a lamp with him.

A small light glimmered in the distance. Good: someone was coming.

'I'm here – over here!' he shouted.

The metal under his hand began to vibrate. Mel felt he should know what that meant but couldn't quite put it together. At least it was brighter now as the lantern was coming closer.

And closer.

Very fast!

The noise built so that the tunnel appeared to be yelling at him to run.

At the last second Mel threw himself sideways

and rolled into a bay between two brick pillars. An underground train roared past, first the hot engine puffing gouts of steam, the engine driver's eyes fixed on the small portion of illuminated track ahead of him, then the string of lit carriages carrying jiggling, jolting commuters under the river. Mel caught a glimpse of face after face staring blankly out of the windows. No one saw him. He could have been a ghost to them. The train rattled on and disappeared to the next station leaving a few glowing sparks behind.

'I'm not a ghost, am I?' Mel slapped his own cheek. Ow. Not dead then.

The time machine. Recalled to his most urgent task before the next service came through, Mel felt his way up and down the tracks. A few yards on, his hands came away with fistfuls of tiny cogs and fragments of glass. The device had gone under the wheels of the train.

'How could I have been so stupid?' Mel asked the air. 'I knew the East London line ran under the river. I should have guessed they'd use the ready-made tunnel rather than dig their own.' All that wonderful artistry, the brilliant technology of the time machine, held by Mel so briefly, was now nothing more than spare parts for watchmakers. He gathered what he could find but decided getting out was more important than coming away with all the pieces. Limping a little, he began the long walk up the line.

Eve stood on the end of the platform at Wapping, the wolf pack weaving around her shins as Cain argued with the stationmaster that he should stop all services using the tunnel.

'I can't do that!' said the portly man, waxed ends of his moustache quivering in the outrage of a small man given an important role. 'They'd take my job away.'

'Whereas I,' said Cain, shoving his face right up against the station controller's, 'will just have your head!'

A train boomed into the station, steam whirling to the ceiling and up through the shaft to the surface. Seeing Eve and the wolves, the passengers who had contemplated getting off at this stop decided to remain on board. The driver didn't wait for the controller to give him his signal but hurriedly chugged on up the line.

'I'm not waiting for this imbecile to see that this is an emergency!' declared Eve, imagining Mel lying injured somewhere in the darkness, alone, thinking no one cared. She jumped down to the track. The wolves leapt past her, Mowgli running close behind.

'We will find him, sister,' he called back to her.

Eve tried to keep up but the wolves' night vision was better than hers. Soon they were little more than a flick of a white hind leg vanishing into the darkness. Then they began howling and barking. They had found something. Eve braced herself. She didn't mind how bad it was as long as Mel was alive. She'd stitch him back together herself if she had to.

'Mel Foster!' she called over the polyphony of ecstatic wolves.

'Eve? Is that you?' The voice sounded so far away she couldn't at first make herself believe she had really heard it.

'Mel Foster! You're alive!' Then she saw him coming out of the gloom, his shock of messy black hair, his bright brown eyes, his funny turned-up nose. The wolves danced at his heels, nipping and licking him, but he didn't seem to mind. Mowgli was helping him walk. 'You are injured?'

He winced. 'Fell from the ceiling.'

'I carry you.' Eve picked him up and tucked him under her arm. 'We had better hurry. That silly man won't stop the trains.' Glancing down the line she could see a little light approaching. 'In fact, I suggest most strongly that we run.'

So that was how Eve returned Mel to 1895: their arrival was heralded by wolves and Mowgli, then she burst out of a tunnel a shade ahead of the noon service from Rotherhithe, carrying Mel under her arm like a loaf of bread. She threw him up to the platform and accepted Cain's aid to haul herself up and out of the path of the engine. The driver had slammed on the brakes, filling the station with an awful squealing noise.

She got clear in the nick of time.

Cain hugged Mel and ruffled his hair, rocking him

to and fro with joy. 'Welcome back, you wretch! For a minute I thought we'd lost you.'

'I've only been gone a minute?' Mel marvelled.

'*Non*, you have been gone a week! You are very bad boy, Mel Foster. We have suffered greatly.'

Mel threw his arms around Eve's waist. 'A week? I'm sorry. Wait – that's exactly how long I spent in 1835! The time machine must have been keeping count somehow. I set it back to twelve.'

'That must be its real time – it would have to have one to keep track of itself or it would just collapse in a heap of its own paradoxes,' said Cain. 'Have you got it with you? I can't wait to examine it.'

Eve didn't want to see that terrible instrument again. It had brought enough trouble to them already without Cain and Abel building more of them, which is certainly what they would do if they got hold of it.

'Um . . . about that.' Mel dug in his pocket and pulled out a handful of sparkling shards and a glitter of metal. He poured them into Cain's palm. 'That's all that's left of the time machine.'

'You broke it?' asked Eve with a smile.

'Unfortunately – or fortunately depending how you look at it – yes, I did. I've concluded that me and time machines really don't mix well together.'

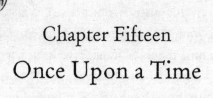

Chapter Fifteen
Once Upon a Time

The first thing Mel did to recover from his ordeal was take a hot bath to wash off the dirt picked up during his adventures and then attend a large tea party for all his friends. The mummy had baked cakes in the shape of clocks and trains. Mel had to admit it was better to eat a train than be run down by one. Mr Copperfield attended, representing the queen. Her Majesty, apparently, was very pleased not to have to surrender to the blackmailer's demands and had returned to her good opinion of the Monster Resistance. Mr Copperfield was now sitting in a corner with his friend, Dr Foster, the two old men trying to figure out how exactly time travel worked.

Good luck with that, thought Mel as he left them to it. He had had enough of paradoxes to last several lifetimes.

Quasimodo was over by the window with the monster fairies. Given a box of pencils by Eve a few days ago to help him learn to write, the French boy had displayed a flair for drawing that had taken them all by surprise. Beret placed on his head at a rakish angle, Quasimodo had already graduated to oils and was currently painting Inky and Nightie's portrait. He was making them look brilliantly ugly, all angles and odd tricks of perspective, completely original but owing something to the stained glass windows of Notre Dame cathedral, Mel thought. If he wasn't much mistaken, Quasimodo was inventing a whole new school of art right here in the monsters' drawing room, which was very appropriate now he thought about it. There was now no question of returning Quasimodo to his own time, so Mel kept his fingers crossed that they hadn't removed a key prop supporting the fabric of the universe by keeping him. Cain had assured Mel that he had found no changes in any history books as a result but, then again – he winked at Mel at this point – they wouldn't know, would they, as they were living in this new timeline?

Constable Wilkins was present too, helping pass round the sandwiches. He was wrapped in a large bath towel, wearing it like a toga, as he had lost his shirt to the mummy when he foolishly agreed to play poker in the kitchen while waiting for the cakes to bake. Mel noticed that Eve was studiously not looking at the young policeman. Ah. It seemed that a lot had happened in the week while he had been away.

'Eve?' Mel sidled up to his best friend, who was listening to Mowgli's tales of the jungle surrounded by five wolves. Five? He saw that Viorica in her she-wolf form was lying with her head resting on Grey Wolf's tummy, as content as Mel had ever seen her.

Eve reached out and took his hand. She kept doing this as if to reassure herself that he was really here. 'You must listen to these stories, Mel Foster. Mowgli has lived an amazing life. His battle with the red dogs – so clever to come out of that alive! The snakes of the lost cities – wonderful!'

'Perhaps you should write a book about it, Mowgli?' suggested Mel.

'A Jungle Book? Who would want to read that?' Mowgli smiled, gesturing round to the civilized trappings of a London house.

'I would, and I think lots of others would too.'

'Maybe I will then.' Mowgli stretched out on the carpet with the wolves, quite at peace now his task was finished. The pack had all been given medals by the queen for their service to the Empire, though Mel thought they might have preferred a meaty bone, and they would be returning first class on the next ship to their homeland. Mel wondered what that passage to India would be like for the other people travelling on board. Interesting, he would wager.

'Eve, may I have a quick word?' asked Mel.

'Of course.'

'Let's go for a walk.' He didn't want Wilkins overhearing their heart-to-heart.

He led Eve into the garden square that lay in front of the house. The family of little children playing with their nurse had got quite used to the monsters living next door. Several ran up to ask Eve to rescue their ball for them, which had got stuck in a tree. This she did by the simple solution of reaching up and plucking it from the branches. They then, naturally, had to stop and play a few rounds of monster-in-the-middle, which Eve had to try very hard to lose as the littlest had great difficulty throwing the ball over her head. Eve loved children. When the nurse collected her charges to go inside, Mel and Eve sat down on a bench. A flock of pigeons landed around them and Eve fed them from a crust she had brought with her from tea.

'I am very fond of pigeons,' she declared.

'Oh, er, good.'

'They know how to come home, like you.'

'That's right.' Mel wasn't exactly sure where that pigeon comment had come from but he had other matters to raise. 'Is everything all right between you and Fred?'

Eve shrugged. 'You were right. He just likes us *because* we look different, not for who we really are under the skin.'

'It's not his fault really, Eve. People take time to adjust to a new idea of normal. At least he does like us; many are scared and don't give us a chance.'

'I think he likes the mummy best. I don't begrudge the mummy that as he hasn't had a special friend for centuries. And I've got you: you're my best friend.'

Mel was flattered but he knew that he couldn't replace Eve's hopes of romance. 'You mustn't give up, Eve. I've been told that you have to kiss a lot of frogs until you find a prince.'

Eve frowned. 'Why would one kiss a frog? Is that a good idea?'

'It's a what-you-ma-call-it – a metaphor. It means that Wilkins is just one fish in a very big sea of possible catches.'

'He is a fish?' Her confusion worsened.

Mel reminded himself that he should speak more plainly if he wanted Eve to understand. 'What I meant to say is that you are the best girl ever and one day some lucky and incredibly clear-sighted person is going to see that and court you. When he does, all I ask is that you don't forget me.'

Eve's shoulders relaxed and her spine straightened with pride. 'You think so?'

'I know so.'

'And you? Will you find a special girl of your own too one day? Someone who looks past snub noses and freckles?'

'Ugh no. I'm not ready for icky stuff, Eve. Not old enough.'

She nodded sagely. 'True. You are too small yet.'

The sun had dipped below the roofs and shadows marched over the gardens taking up occupation for the night.

'Time to go in?' said Mel.

In the hallway, Jacob Marley emerged from a wall to greet them.

'I cannot tell you, young sir, how delighted I am to see you back safely,' the ghost confided, wafting Mel's cap and Eve's bonnet to the hatstand like a waltzing couple.

Mel waited for Eve to return to the drawing room before speaking. This was one part of his adventure he had not told anyone. 'I'm really sorry, Mr Marley, if I caused you trouble in the past.'

Marley grew a little whiter, a fraction more solid as he flushed with the ghost equivalent of pleasure. 'Not at all. You may have sometimes forgotten to wipe your shoes on entry but such things are mere nothings in the face of the prospect of losing you forever.'

'That's not quite what I meant. Do you remember me, from your other life, I mean?'

Marley faded slightly as he cast his mind back. 'No, I'm afraid not. All that seems very distant now, mere echoes in eternity. Did we meet?'

'Briefly.'

Marley looked away. 'I suppose I wasn't very nice to you, was I?'

'Not as such. And I think I might have contributed to you catching the chill that carried you off.' There: he had confessed.

'Ah, is that all?' Marley tried to pat his shoulder but his hand just passed through Mel. 'Nothing to fret over, young sir. You did me a service. If I had stayed alive any longer my chains and cashboxes would have grown with every passing year and I would be contemplating yet worse regrets for my sins than I do already. It was good I went when I did, never doubt that.'

'And when do you stop . . .' Mel couldn't think of quite the right word for ghostliness, 'being like this?'

'When I've settled my debts to those I wronged in my lifetime.'

Mel looked more closely at Marley's chain. Was it not a few links shorter than when he had first met the ghost?

'That's right. I see you understand. You may have caused trouble for me in the past but now you are helping me mend my ways.' Marley curled his chain over his arm like a bride carrying her long veil. 'Once upon a time I was the most miserly man in London and now I'm . . . not.' With a smile, Jacob Marley wafted up through the ceiling, indulging in a little happy cry of 'Doom!' to keep up his spirits.

Much relieved, Mel stood alone in the hall for a moment. The grandfather clock ticked reassuringly, the minute hand moving forward just as it should. Despite everything, he was back in one piece and it was time he rejoined his friends at the tea party. Quasimodo was going to paint Eve next. The artist had said he found Eve's scars inspiring. To Quasimodo, she was the most beautiful face he had ever seen. Mel couldn't wait to see the results.

Well, actually, he could wait. He would never wish to live in anything but the present ever again.

Resting in the silent depths of the Thames, moored over the tunnel that carried trains under the riverbed, a submarine waited for new orders. A door to the captain's cabin opened and the Inventor stepped out.

'We're done here,' he announced, folding a newspaper under his arm. The headline declared in big black letters that all the valuables had been recovered and returned to their owners. The fruit thief's robbery spree was over, thanks to the Monster Resistance. Another plot foiled, but the Inventor, unlike his hero Napoleon, knew when it was time to make a tactical retreat. 'Take us out to sea.'

'Aye aye, captain.' The first mate rang a bell, warning the crew that the vessel was about to begin another of its voyages.

The *Nautilus* powered up its revolutionary electric motors and purred seawards, leaving not even a wake behind.

'Until next time, Mel Foster,' murmured the Inventor, returning to his desk where he drew up his plans for world domination. 'And I promise you, my boy: you won't see me coming.'

I am Cat Royal

Orphan, adventurer, actress . . .

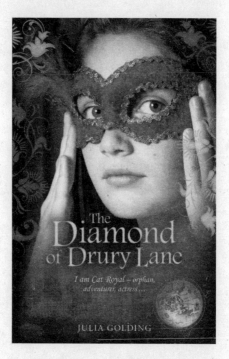

Winner of the Nestlé Children's Book Prize

Read all of Cat's adventures: